D1476432

If You Are Reading This Then Drink Water

Daragh Fleming

RIVERSONG
BOOKS

An Imprint of Sulis International Press
Los Angeles | London

ISBN (print): 978-1-946849-74-8
ISBN (eBook): 978-1-946849-75-5

Published by Riversong Books
An Imprint of Sulis International
Los Angeles | London

www.sulisinternational.com

Table of Contents

For Kev & Age

Absurdity:

The act of looking for meaning in a world that has none.

Introduction

You'd be dead fairly quickly without water. I'm sure you already know that. Water is fundamental. Water is the essence of life. Water is so powerful it can both keep you alive and kill you, depending on the amount. Water is God in a certain sense.

The average human being is advised to drink two litres of the stuff every day. Two litres. That's not much, and yet a lot of us fail to do so. A lot of us like to think ourselves special, or unique or important yet we can't meet the water requirements of an average person.

If you want to be great at something, you have to try to be great at everything. You can't expect more than mediocre if you can't even attain mediocrity in water consumption. Today's the day to start. Shed the rags of mediocrity. Begin the road to greatness today. Drink more water. Drink more than two litres, you dehydrated gowl.

These stories were written in a fog of dehydration. They'll make sense to a brain seduced by thirst. They'll seem fucking nonsensical to the hydrated mind. If you're reading this and you don't get what's going on, then rest assured that you're drinking enough H2O. But if you find yourself reading this book, this collection, and it seems to make sense then you need to drink more water.

Enjoy yourselves.

The Bus to Boston

Scents of heavy, flirtatious diesel were the olfactory backdrop to New York, New York. For me, the urgency of the city was its defining characteristic. The charm of this concrete jungle was its ability to humble anyone. Everywhere people hurried and hurtled through the streets, uninterested in any other purpose aside from their own. There was a sense of madness to it. Not the same madness that'd rise off the bog lands back home, it was more uniform than that. The crowds within the bus station at Grand Central Terminal were no different. I forged a path through the throngs of weary travellers. The pace of the place gave the historic station an incomparable energy. You'd imagine someone would look down on the place and think of ants. Even at this late point in the evening, the famous terminal was still a hive of activity. The bus to Boston left at 11:30, giving me 20 minutes to find my way to its departure gate.

The queue waiting for me at Gate 13A had me worrying I wouldn't be able to sit on my lonesome. I had assumed the bus to Boston on a Sunday evening would be quiet. However, it now looked as though every seat would be filled. The concrete block of a Greyhound bus sat idly in the bay, waiting to make the almost 4-hour journey to South Station in Boston. The driver checked tickets with glazed eyes as myself and the rest of the passengers boarded the monster of a bus. The seats rose from the floor like tombstones in the darkness of the carriage. I sat near the back, by the window so that I could look out on the roads as we meandered to Boston. It wasn't long before a man in his mid-20s sat next to me, and his friend of around the same age sat across the aisle from him.

The bitter fragrance of unwashed skin was mild but unmistakable. Both of the men were skinny and pale. The one sat next to me had a close-to-shaved head while his friend had shoulder-length, brown hair. Both were quite smiley, and you could sense their excitement radiating from their skin. The energy between the pair was restless, as they chatted amongst themselves un-apologetically on the quiet bus. As the bus floated through the giants of Manhattan towards the highway, I waited for my neighbour to spark up conversation. I didn't have to wait long.

"What has you going to Boston, my man?" I couldn't place his accent, but I knew it wasn't a New York one. I couldn't focus on anything besides the fact that he hadn't showered in some time.

"Ah I live there, only came down to New York for the weekend." I could feel the words stumbling from my lips.

"Whoa! What accent is that? Where are you from, bro?" He nudged his friend across the aisle, clearly quite entertained by my strange way of speaking.

"I'm Irish, man. Just over this side of the world for the summer." There was a seediness to these boys that had my gut asking questions. Something about the situation had me feeling uneasy. Not wanting to give into prejudice, I attempted to be as amicable as possible.

"No way, man. That's awesome! We're from Florida, bro. I'm Mike and that's Tyler. We're heading to Providence to my grandma's place. It was time for us to get out of Florida and start fresh."

"Ah nice. Florida looks cool man, I was gonna try and get there this summer too but I might not be able. Did it take ye long to get up here?"

There was a pause as Mike tried to decipher the meaning through my alien accent. It eventually clicked into place as I repeated some of the key words.

"Ah, right. Sorry man, your accent is like music. We've been travelling for 4 days now. We hitchhiked and got buses all the way to New York and now we're almost there. Not really sure how we'll manage to get to Providence once we get to Boston, but we'll figure it out, ain't that right Tyler?"

Tyler released a goofy chuckle and said, "Totally, bro". I forced a smile and hoped that I didn't look as uneasy as I felt.

Mike included me in the conversation between him and Tyler a little bit more often than I would have encouraged. He asked about Ireland, and the women in Ireland, and drinking. He seemed genuinely interested in getting to know me and the discomfort I felt slowly eased up as our bus rumbled through the night. Unprompted, Mike began showing me pictures on his phone after a while. There was a lick of pride in his face as he looked to me for validation as he swiped through. His collection consisted of multiple pictures of himself wielding various fire arms. There was one of him with some sort of handgun (I had no idea of the make and he didn't seem certain either). There was a photo of him in a back garden wielding an assault rifle at Floridian sunset. The next picture was clearly taken on the same day, except this time Mike was topless harnessing a bow & arrow, posed in a side profile, so the full draw of the bow was captured. He was wearing some camouflage three-quarter length shorts. It was by far, the most American thing I'd ever seen but I kept that observation to myself.

The weapon photos were separated, in no particular order, by naked photos of Mike's most recent ex-girlfriend. It was bizarre to watch as Mike scrolled from the picture of him with the bow, to an unflattering picture of a Latino woman in her early 20s, back to a picture of Mike with a handgun and so on. What was even more bizarre was that Mike didn't comment on, or get embarrassed by the fact that these pictures were in the mix. I felt pangs of guilt and pity for the girl in the picture, who'd no idea that her ex fella would be showing her tits to a near stranger on a bus to Boston. Tyler peered over Mike's right shoulder, quietly admiring each photo. The feeling of unease lurched into my stomach once again, making me feel light-headed and warm.

Not long after Mike showed me his insane gallery, the bus driver pulled in for a pit stop outside a gas station on the side of the deserted highway. We were just about halfway to Boston. The 2 Floridians decided to go to the nearby supermarket for some food. They asked me if I wanted to come, and when I declined they asked if I wanted anything. I also declined. Their effort to get on my good side hadn't gone unnoticed, but my gut told me there was some sort of agenda driving this.

After 15 minutes of peace, the two lads came back to the bus, carrying with them a large bucket of cold fried chicken and a 2-liter bottle of Mountain Dew. They encouraged me to help myself to both, but again, I declined. I had brought my own water from New York and took a timely swig to reaffirm my decline. At this stage it was almost 2AM and my sole focus was on getting home to some much-needed sleep. Sleep on this bus was out of the question and over the next hour of the journey to Boston, I was destined to learn far too much about the lifestyle of Mike and Tyler.

They began to talk about the crack days. This isn't some code word for some benign thing. Mike and Tyler began chatting about the months and years they had spent addicted to crack in Florida. I felt that this was the big reveal that my subconscious had somehow been expecting, and had been warning me about via massive discomfort throughout the entire journey. They spent countless afternoons in the balmy heat of the Floridian sun, smoking crack in the back yard of a mother that was, to quote 'sick of Mike's shit'. Mike and Tyler were ex-crackheads, and it made total sense. It explained their impulsive exodus from their home state. It explained their seemingly unfocused existence, their hygiene, the colour of the teeth they had left, and their untethered sense of style, and social awareness. The two dudes were only 'clean' from crack for just over a month, a claim both seemed equally proud of.

"I wouldn't say I'll never do it again, but it feels good to be sober, man. Just liquor and weed from here on," Tyler nodded at me, his jaw swinging as loosely as his understanding of sobriety. Mike spoke about crack with a passion, and it was clear from his description of how it used to make him feel that he wasn't out of the wheelhouse of cravings just yet. Unfortunately for me, the revelation about their shared addiction to crack wasn't where it ended, and about 90 minutes away from Boston, I found myself in an unprovoked conversation about religion.

"So, you're a Catholic, right? That's pretty big in Ireland?" Mike seemed more serious now than he had been all night. He had turned to face me dead on, and the shadows of the bus made it impossible to see where he was looking. The unease pulsed through me to the rhythm of my pacing heart.

"Era, I was raised Catholic alright, but I wouldn't be practicing it, like. It has a bad rep at home at the moment and I was never too religious," I delivered my reply along a nervous laugh.

"Too right, brother. Christianity has been going wrong for centuries, my man. I'm a Satanist myself.

So's Tyler. It's definitely a better path," If Mike could have seen my face in the dark he'd have seen the colour drain from it entirely. Mike hadn't even lowered his voice to tell me of his loyalty to the Devil. A revelation he was most definitely proud of.

"…oh, yeah?" The two friends stared at me in the dark of the bus.

"Yes, sir. And to be honest with you, I think you'd really get into it if you gave it a try, you seem like you're on the same wavelength as us."

The words hung there in the idleness of that packed bus. They floated above all the sleeping passengers and along the quiet highway that lead to Boston and beyond across the ocean to home and I imagined that somewhere on that small island, there was a parish priest who'd sensed there was a countryman in danger. The words pierced into my soul. I wasn't so sleepy anymore. I'd been shooketh awake by the absurdity of it all. I had purposely disclosed very little about myself to these strange men. And yet this man, this ex-crack-addicted Satanist, felt that he had gotten to know me well enough in the 3 hours we'd been sat next to each other to say that he thought I'd enjoy the lifestyle and ethos outlined by the Satanic Church.

In the most deadpan and sincere way I could, I looked Mike directly in the eye and replied, "I really fucking doubt it, pal," and put an earphone into my left ear, to signify the conversation was over. Mike didn't register the social cue whatsoever and attempted to convince me of the merits of Satanism, to which he got no response. By the time we got to South Station in Boston, I had unwillingly learned quite a lot about the sect and its culture, and made a mental note to read into it at a later stage, for academic purposes of course.

As we disembarked the tired bus and collected our luggage from the undercarriage. I was shocked that the two homeless Floridians didn't ask if they could stay in my house for the night. It was a request I'd been expecting and had readied myself to sprint in the direction of the taxi rank at a moment's notice. Instead Mike told me to "Stay safe out there, brother", and Tyler made Devil's horns with his left hand against his forehead in silence. The gesture made me question whether they had been serious or whether they were trying to prank me to pass the time. I reassured myself that they had to be serious, given the sincerity that Mike had displayed when he claimed I could really enjoy Satanism. I turned and walked to the curb where my Uber awaited, completely exhausted from the long and bizarre journey. The driver asked where I was going and I gave him the address and then we whispered through a quiet Boston.

Pipe down over there now, Martin
You haven't even your jocks on yet.
There'll be no feeding swans today
If you don't behave

Magpie Apologist

The common pigeon is similar to the average human in lots of ways. A pigeon can recognize itself in a mirror, one of only 6 species on the entire planet that can do that. So in a way, pigeons are on the same level as human beings. A pigeon mates for life, and so a pigeon's biggest fear is dying alone. This is the biggest common ground shared between man and pigeon. There's an unspoken affinity between the two species. There isn't a man who knows more about this affinity than Jinty Flanagan.

Jinty was a well-established ornithologist, who held expert knowledge on the lifestyle and behavioural normalities of the Eurasian Magpie, ironically enough. As a child he even had a pet magpie named Jerry, who got shredded by his father's lawn mower during the summer of 1998. Although Jerry's death was untimely, Jinty's fascination with the bird remained strong and he made studying the magpie his life's passion. Therefore, it came as quite a disappointment when Jinty learned that he could talk to pigeons.

It was the morning after the night before. Jinty Flanagan's head was the inside of a vacuum cleaner as he winced his way through the rain. His t-shirt was a saturated bog as he followed South Mall onto the semipedestrianised Grand Parade and made his was toward the blue McDonald's which lay on the far end of the same street. The Peace Park opened up on his left, an open, concrete public park with decorative squares of grass and flowers spread sporadically around it. He had the lean of a man who wasn't sure of himself. His limbs were pointed and unsure of where to be. Once Jinty made it inside the fast-food restaurant, he combed over his drenched hair with his left hand in an attempt to cover his badly receding hairline. There wasn't a fool in sight who saw nor cared. He used the self-service terminal to order a double cheeseburger, some nuggets and some much-needed water. Jinty suffered at a nearby table and scoffed down the cheap food, trying to nurse his sore head back to normality. He forced the water down, his body still gripped by the reluctance of the hangover. As he exited the restaurant, he noticed that the rain had stopped, not that it mattered now.

Jinty's brother, Clarence, had agreed to collect him outside at around 11:30, which by then was only a few minutes away. He leant against the wall of the establishment, breathing deep to try and overcome to building urge to vomit. He leaned there with his eyes closed, arms folded. The lick of 40 was fast approaching Jinty. Wrinkles were creeping up on him like dusk on a summer's night.

Only steps away, a cluster of pigeons, bobbed and weaved, eyeing the floor for morsels of food that passers-by may have dropped. Jinty eyed them up, enjoying the thought of kicking one into the air. It was an intrusive thought that he often had, and was one of the few that he welcomed. One pigeon, a stout, big-chested young fellow, wandered from the group towards Jinty. It carried more confidence in its stride than a young fella trying to get the shift of a Saturday down the Mangala. Jinty looked around him in feverish excitement, suddenly aware of his opportunity to actually kick the isolated pigeon. Noticing that the street was as empty as the local nightclub, Jinty wound up his leg to punt the fat bird. A high-pitched, and extremely Cork voice shouting at him, interrupting the forward swing of his size 10.

"Don't you even think about it, you long bastard!" Jinty froze. His right leg still poised to kick. Jinty peered around the street to find the source of the high-pitched squeal but the area was still as barren as his step-dad.

"Down here, you sausage". Jinty looked down, his face now stretched in horrified confusion. The pigeon ruffled its feathers and twisted its head in a very pigeon-like movement.

"Kick me and you won't step outside again without being shat all over, get me?"

The pigeon jerked its head forward, almost in mockery. Jinty was stunned entirely. Some aggressive car honking from the road snapped him out of it and he turned to see Clarence hanging out the driver-side window of his grey Opel Corsa, shouting for him. Jinty ran to the car, still in horror from the talking pigeon.

"Clar, that pigeon was talking to me!"

"Oh fuck me, Mam wasn't talking shite. You are back on the psychedelics. Stop listening to Joe Rogan, you'll have no brain left soon."

"No man, I swear that pigeon shouted at me 'cause I tried to kick it."

"What in the fuck? Why were you gonna kick it? G'way now, Jinty and don't annoy me. You're a pure pisshead."

Clarence turned up the radio to drown Jinty out. Jinty sat, his forehead wrinkled in thought. Maybe he had taken something the previous night. His memory was a mess of a fog. By the time they reached the house, Jinty had shrugged it off as a session-related hallucination and tried to forget about what happened. He clambered into bed and tried to forget that he'd ever mentioned that a pigeon tried to fight him.

Jinty didn't go hard on the session too often. He enjoyed his work and treated it with extreme reverence. In all honesty, Jinty loved nothing more than to get in the lab and engage in some cutting-edge research about magpies. The passion he showed for his work was only matched by his expertise. His current project aimed to understand the biochemistry of the magpie's brain to see if an intervention could be developed to stop the birds from eating the unhatched eggs of lesser species. It was against their very nature, but the intervention would improve the situation of countless other species. The ends justified the means, in Jinty's eyes.

One evening in mid-November, Jinty was shutting up the lab on his own. He had sent Bridget, his assistant, home early as there wasn't much left to be done that would require the both of them. He locked the door and stepped outside into the brisk air. The cold hand of winter was already gripping the evening firmly. The industrial estate's car park was more or less empty. It had just turned 5PM so there was still some daylight left as the shadows of dusk slowly settled in.

Before Jinty could take a single step, a weighted object silently struck his right shoulder. Caught by surprise, Jinty startled before peered down to find the unmistakable whiteness of bird shit on his jacket.

"Oh for fuck sake!" Jinty exhaled. He scanned the surround area to see if he could find the culprit, not that there was anything he could do. At first he saw nothing at all, but then in his peripheral, he saw something. A large pigeon, with long grey wings, had circled back into view and was now descending towards Jinty. There was nowhere for Jinty to hide. The pigeon was too fast, and the car was too far away to take cover. As the pigeon peeled in just overhead, it bellowed, in a thick Glaswegian accent.

"Fucking Magpie-apologist!" and unloaded another massive load onto Jinty. This time it was a direct hit and smashed into the top of Jinty's head, exploding all over his hair and down onto his face. The Scottish pigeon flew off into the November dusk laughing heartily, leaving Jinty covered in white bird waste and feeling extremely confused. Still shaking, he sat into his car and took a deep breath before turning on the engine and driving home. Pigeons were definitely talking to him. Jinty pondered whether he should have himself admitted to a hospital based on that. As he pulled up to the curb outside his apartment, he concluded that he'd better make sure that the common pigeon was indeed talking to him before making any life-altering decisions. Luckily, he knew just where to go.

The following Saturday morning Jinty stepped off the bus onto Grand Parade. He found his stomach doing somersaults, but wasn't surprised that he was nervous. He was, after all, about to enter the Peace Park, the Mecca of pigeons. It was 9:30AM yet the park was surprisingly busy, and there was no shortage of pigeons. They bobbed and weaved and hopped all over. It had rained the night before and so the smell of wet concrete made the place feel dirtier than it was. He entered through the main archway that opened into the expanse of the park. Jinty noticed almost instantly, how noisy the park was. It sounded like hundreds of people were there, murmuring and chatting, yet there could only have been 30 people at most, and the majority of them were a good 20 yards away. It was only as he approached the hordes of pigeons that he understood; It wasn't the voices of people he was hearing, it was the chattering of wild pigeons. The park sounded like an exciting cocktail party. A group of female pigeons nearby were talking about their chicks at home. Several arrogant males were arguing about who had shat on the most statues that morning. Most of the pigeons were shouting at passers-by demanding food.

"Throw us down some bread there, you tall eejit." A grey pigeon with a shimmering green chest stood at Jinty's feet with its head tilted towards him so that its left eye was staring directly into Jinty's.

"Eh, I don't have any, pal." Jinty shrugged his shoulders in apology. He was painfully aware that he was talking to a bird.

No sooner had the words left his mouth that every pigeon within earshot fell silent and turned toward Jinty, in what can only be described as stunned disbelief. For what felt like an eternity, the pigeons stared at Jinty, and Jinty stared at the pigeons. The silence was eventually broken as the pigeons broke into a panicked hysteria. Pigeons scrambled left and right, screaming "What the fuck?", and "Holy shit!". Many more took to the skies, releasing guttural pigeon-roars as they did so. Other humans passing by just saw a man shrugging in the middle of a frenzy of pigeons and assumed the man was unwell. Jinty, however, was frozen in place, completely stunned by the fact that pigeons could understand him, and he pigeons. He was all but ready to have himself sectioned when a deep, powerful voice boomed up from the ground.

"Silence!" The single order was enough to put an immediate end to the hysteria going on around Jinty. The crowd of birds parted, making way for one of the broadest pigeons Jinty had ever laid eyes on. He was followed up by 6 other pigeons who were clearly much older. It became apparent from the reaction of the horde that Jinty was now in the presence of a very important pigeon indeed. The colossal bird took its time before speaking again, basking in the silence he had instilled.

"We are a people of faith, human. We believe in the higher power outlined in our sacred text. Written by our ancestors long ago, it has guided our societies throughout the world."

The Pigeon King paused as the crowd stirred in support.

"Our scriptures tell of the coming of The One. It is said that The One shall not be of our kind, but will come and help us vanquish our forsaken enemy. I have spoken with our tribe's elders," he gestured to the six older pigeons behind him with his muscular wing, "Their interpretation of the texts suggest that a human named John shall one day be granted the ability to communicate with Pigeon-kind, and that this is a sign of the Precursor. This John, is the PiJohn of our sacred prophecy." The great pigeon paused again, and there was complete silence amongst the birds. Some of the birds could be heard whispering prayers near the back. Passers-by on the now quite busy Grand Parade walkway, glanced at the strange man staring at the mass of pigeons as they hurried along the street.

"So tell me, human, are you The One, the true Pi-John?" He leaned in, now listening intently.

"Eh, fucking hell, I dunno, man. This is mental altogether. My name is John alright but the lads call me Jinty. Are you sure I'm not just losing my mind like? Nobody can talk to pigeons in fairness."

The Pigeon King stared at Jinty, his beady right eye weighing up the man that towered over him. The elders murmured amongst themselves for a moment and then turned to nod reassuringly at the King.

"There is no running from fate, human. Be it PiJohn or PiJinty, it is clear. You are The One. You shall help Pigeon-kind vanquish the Hellish Magpie and rid this world of their plague. You are The One!" There was a deafening roar of celebration following the King's revelation. Jinty's heart was beating rapidly, as he now realized these birds believed him to be some sort of messianic figure.

The celebrations were interrupted by a single, unique squawk that emanated from the throat of the king. It was a sound Jinty had never heard a pigeon make before, and it filled him with a deep sense of foreboding. Almost as if they had been waiting, the countless pigeons leapt into the air briefly before finding a place to perch upon the shoulders, arms, legs and head of Jinty. Several pigeons hovered next to Jinty and began to shout "Heave!". The Pigeon King appeared in Jinty's left periphery, and Jinty heard the bird assure him that everything would be fine. The pigeons, which were now latched onto Jinty, started to flap and pull and drag wildly. Slowly, Jinty felt his weight lighten as his feet left the floor. Suddenly he was 10 feet in the air, 50 feet in the air, and before long, he was soaring over the rooves of the building on Washington Street which ran perpendicular to Grand Parade. The awestruck people on Grand Parade and further afield watched on in disbelief as a man was dragged into the sky and out of sight by a massive flock of pigeons.

*LOCAL "PIGEON WHISPERER" STILL MISSING
AFTER PEACE-PARK PANDEMONIUM*

The words lifted off the front page of the Echo as Jinty read them. He scratched at his uneven beard and smiled before tearing up the paper and tossing the pieces into the fire near-by. Pulling his pigeon-feather cloak around him for warmth, he gazed around at the hundreds of birds that inhabited the cave with him as they settled down for the night. Soon the war would begin. Jinty just hoped humankind wouldn't get caught up in it.

Did you like my picture?

No.

Why not?

Not really on Instagram.

You're strange, boy

Omniscient Nostril Rupture

It was a bad cup of coffee. It tasted like the beans had been left in the bottom of an ashtray. Too bitter and sour to tolerate. Still, Joe drank it. It was a warm distraction on a rather crisp October morning. The coffee shop was quiet, now that the clock had slinked past 9 o'clock and the morning rushers had begun their day. Still, the hum of excited chatter filled the small cafe, complimenting the scent of poorly prepared South American coffee. Joe thoughtlessly mixed his black coffee with a wooden stirrer as he observed the usual wheels spin. The male barista prepared a macchiato to go, and there was a man in a suit by the far window talking loudly on his phone. She was sat where she always sat. The sunlight kissed her through the window behind her. The light illuminated the cartilage of her ears like heat lamps. Her blonde hair was tied into the most perfect, untidy ponytail, fingers hammering away at the keyboard in front of her. The latte she ordered was already going cold, as always. Joe admired her routine, her discipline. He despised that she could drink cold coffee.

He often wondered if she had noticed him. He knew she hadn't. In all the times he had sat here, and she there, Joe hadn't once crossed this girl's mind. He may as well have been invisible. Although only 20 feet divided them, it may as well have been an entire ocean. She thought about her characters, and her plot (which needed work) and about some guy named Trevor whom she liked but who didn't seem to like her back. She thought about calling her mom, and when the rent was due, and what she'd do for dinner, but never about Joe. The male barista thought about how much of a loser Joe appeared to be. He had noticed Joe coming in every day and had caught wind of how often he glanced at the gorgeous blonde. He had a lot to think about that, didn't he? Joe didn't mind that, since he knew what the male barista got up to down by the docks with some people his wife might not want to hear about. He'd a strange fetish for a seemingly straight-shooter.

People really need to be more careful with their thoughts, Joe considered. Very silly leaving personal details floating around unprotected. The girl stirred, and began packing up her things. She had class soon. Joe waited for his moment to bump into her at the door, as he did every so often. He fumbled on his phone as he made towards the door. The girl let out a noticeable sigh of frustration, as Joe obliviously blocked the exit. He looked up from his phone with believable surprise and a slight smile that whispered his apology.

"Oh, excuse me, I didn't see you there." He pushed the door open, gesturing with his left paw for her to pass through. She walked passed him without saying a word, and the scent of her familiar shampoo hit his nostrils.

"I really am sorry, I wouldn't normally miss someone as pretty as you." The words were hanging in the air between them before he could stop himself. His stomach dropped into his jocks and he almost choked on the heart in his mouth. The silence that followed was deafening. To Joe's surprise, the girl turned back to him, looking him up and down. She gave him a wide, closed smile and said "Aw, that's ok, hun," with a light giggle, before turning on her left heel and making her way down a bustling Oliver Plunkett Street, her step as light as her laughter. Joe's stomach lurched with delight. They had finally talked. She now knew he existed and he couldn't help but feel hopeful. He allowed himself a quiet fist-pump of celebration outside the corner coffee shop. He didn't see the barista inside the window rolling his eyes at the cringey man outside. Joe's hope was shattered within a breath, as he was forced to hear the girl's initial thought louder than any other on that lively street.

What a fucking creep!

The crushing weight of humiliation is even heavier when nobody else knows why you're humiliated. The words had hit him like a bullet to the shoulder. The coffee shop girl didn't know. She thought she'd ended the interaction quite amicably, and she technically had. But Joe knew what she had really thought after their interaction and it broke his heart. Like all sensible people do, Joe convinced himself that this girl, this person that he had taken fancy to, wasn't actually that special. Still, knowing what people really think of you isn't easy. What people think is unfiltered, unedited. It's real. It's what they truly, and initially believe. It's their truth. Joe knew what most people really thought of him, whether he liked it or not.

This unfortunate ability led Joe to be quite the anxious fellow. He couldn't go to the shops for milk without giving himself a good talking to. His hands were always red-raw from the wringing and nervous scratching. His psychiatrist had prescribed him some potent anti-anxiety medication, based on his severe and seemingly irrational fear of what people thought about him. Of course, Joe hadn't mentioned that he could hear people's thoughts. He knew how it sounded and he didn't want to be sent away somewhere against his will. Therapy wasn't even worthwhile considering he could also hear the therapist's thoughts. She didn't listen to much of what Joe said, rather she had a set list of responses that seemed to work in every situation. It was both impressive, and deeply disturbing, how good the doctor was at being in two places at once.

Then again, everyone Joe came across had disturbed him to some degree. People thought some wicked and admittedly creative things. Some were conscious, controlled and on purpose. People sometimes went into vivid and horrid detail of the different ways they'd like to kill various people in their lives, and even strangers. People had inappropriate thoughts all day, every day, and Joe could hear them all. Sometimes Joe even wondered if he should report some of the people because of how deeply disturbing their thoughts were about killing spouses, children, and family members. But then he'd conveniently recall the plot of Minority Report and concluded it wasn't such a good idea. That, coupled with the anxiety of walking into a police station and explaining himself, ensured he'd never acted on his instinct to help, and he'd been able to hear thoughts since he could remember.

It came as no surprise then that Joe hated superhero movies and anything to do with superpowers. It was too unrealistic, too unbearably straight forward. Not one superhero in the course of history had ever had anxiety, or depression as a result of their powers, or what their powers let them do. There was never a superhero on TV that had some sort of mental health issue, not one. Telepaths in the movies always seem so on top of their shit. In reality, all telepathy does is confirm when people don't like you, and if they do like you, it forces you to experience first-hand as they slowly begin to dislike you in very specific and relentless detail. Reading thoughts might seem like a cool thing to be able to do, but when you're already anxious, it makes your whole life a living nightmare.

After the incident with the girl at the coffee shop, Joe didn't leave his house for days. He lumbered around, unshaven with his back up to anything said to him. The mother worried. He could hear her pottering away, the thoughts chattering and abrasive in her mind, gnawing away at her as she went about her business. She often worried, and Joe marvelled at her ability to mask it. He admired her for it. Eventually she started prodding at him verbally and Joe agreed that he'd go back to Dr.

Moynihan for a check-in, more so to keep her happy than anything else. None of the family knew about his ability, about his curse. In fact, nobody on Earth knew. He'd have loved to relieve himself of the unyielding stress. He'd have loved to tell Dr. Moynihan how torturous it is to be able to hear the most personal, twisted, heartbreaking, corrupt and terrible thoughts of strangers, and how it was even more unbearable to hear the thoughts of those he knew and loved. He just wanted to let it all out and figure a way to turn off his ability and have some peace, even if just for a few minutes. But he couldn't tell anyone, because nobody would understand. Instead, he just told the doctor that he felt uncomfortable in social situations, and she prescribed the meds that Joe never really took, and sometimes sold to the junkies down the Wharf on a Sunday evening. They'd line up for the things because if you took enough of them at once you got a good buzz from them. Joe often made decent coin off his meds when the demand was there.

Joe's appointment was on a Tuesday morning. He arrived at the clinic, 15 minutes early, as always. The morning was bright and vivid and felt like Christmas. The clinic was located on Union Quay and overlooked the branch of the River Lee that curled around the College of Commerce, an adult learning centre on the river's bank. The murky water sparkled in the sunlight as Joe pushed through the door to the lobby of Dr. Moynihan's office.

He kept his headphones on, with the music turned up loud to drown out the thoughts of the many people that were fluttering around the place. It was a psychiatric outpatient department of the University Hospital, and so there were many student psychiatrists shadowing doctors. It had always amazed Joe how much people bluff and don't pay attention, and how unbelievably carless people could be when it came to other people's problems. Joe had found out on his very first day coming to the clinic that doctor-patient confidentiality was nothing more than a thing people said, which he could tell from the thoughts of the three individuals that had been in the break room. The problems of patients were discussed, and mocked and laughed at without remorse.

For Joe, coming to the clinic was more of a courtesy than anything else. It kept his over-involved parents happy, and it kept the chance of in-house treatment at bay if he appeared to be stable and consistent.

Joe stood up 5 seconds before he was called by the receptionist. An instinctive habit he often couldn't shake, but what most people just thought to be 'good timing'. He smiled at the receptionist and made a face that implied, "What are the chances?" whilst shrugging his shoulders. The receptionist laughed.

"Dr. Moynihan is in Suite 3", he said, looking back down at the screen in front of him, thinking about his golden retriever, Lola. She was in for a neutering, as it were.

Joe knocked twice and entered the room. He was greeted by Dr. Moynihan, along with two much younger doctors sitting to her left on a small couch. Dr. Moynihan's gave one of her on-brand narrow, eyeless smiles, which was accompanied by the overeager grins of two loon-faced student doctors. Reading the room wasn't a skill one could learn from a book. One of them was already panicking about whether she looked 'doctor-ish' enough, the other had already diagnosed Joe with borderline personality disorder. Joe sat into the grey armchair he always sat in and faced the three doctors and their thoughts.

The session went on as it usually did. Dr. Moynihan offered Joe some water, which he accepted and used to wet his lips when they went dry from talking for too long. The doctor used her probes whilst not really paying attention, Joe talked about some of the things that had made him anxious lately, sidestepping the fact that it was all a result of being able to hear people think. The nervous girl was too focused on looking the part for Joe to actually keep her attention and she kept asking him to repeat what he had just said. Annoying. The other student had clearly gotten into psychiatry for the wrong reasons. He kept internally accusing Joe of making things up, being a snowflake, and not being resilient enough. He kept thinking about how Joe needed to 'grow a pair'. The added detail of a trust fund wanker accusing him of faking made Joe begin to lose his patience.

The thoughts of this broad-chested student were so intrusive that Joe lost his own train of thought several times. Dr. Moynihan even seemed concerned by this and straightened herself up, sensing something was off.

"Is everything okay, Joseph? You seem distracted."

"Yeah, I'm fine, really. It's just do you ever get that thing where something is niggling away at you and you just can't seem to get around it? Like when you're watching TV and there are people having a conversation nearby, and you can't help but focus on the conversation even though you want to concentrate on the TV?"

"Of course, that's a perfectly normal experience, Joseph", Joe could feel the doctor loose interest again as her focus switched back off. The student's thoughts, however, his selfish, self-involved thoughts, were so loud now in Joe's head that he could barely hear anything else. It had never been this bad with anyone before, and Joe didn't know if he'd be able to bear it much longer. He felt light-headed and squinted as his vision became narrowed and blurry. Joe began to think louder himself. He wrapped his own thoughts around the students in an attempt to drown him out, to suffocate the horrible things he was thinking. Joe imagined his own thought-stream coiling around the student doctor's thoughts, squeezing tighter and tighter around them. He imagined that the louder his thoughts got, the tighter the grip got. It seemed to be working too, because the student's thoughts were becoming less audible. Even the student himself seemed to be shrinking into his chair. With one last effort, Joe screamed, *Fuck off you prick!* in his mind as loud as he possibly could, and the thoughts of the student disappeared instantly.

A lash of warmth hit the left shoulder and chest of Dr. Moynihan with some force, and a look of complete shock washed over her face, draining all colour from her pointed cheeks. The student doctor, the one who had been unbearably inconsiderate with his thoughts, had already slumped back in the armchair he occupied, crimson life funnelling from his nostrils and ears, at an almost unbelievable rate. The other student doctor let out a terrible, guttural scream which pierced the air, as she ran from the room. Joe was splattered with a good deal of blood across his face and chest but he just sat there. Gazing at the dead student doctor, Joe was in shock at what had just happened but also found himself engrossed is his discovery. The burden of hearing people's thoughts did have an off switch, although it was a costly price to pay.

Lovely, creamy, gorgeous, pint of black
The taste of an Irish winter
Down the Southern coast
Fuck off you, with your IPA
And don't even think about taking a sip
Before she settles

Joyride

The old man had a penchant for tinkering away in the garage. Some nights he'd be up at all hours, fumbling and prodding at some new project. I couldn't tell you how many times we'd been woken by the fire alarm going off, the old man howling as he extinguished his mistakes. He considered himself an inventor but he was really a pensioner who had more time than he'd bargained for with an inability to sit still. Nevertheless, he came through for me the morning my car door wouldn't close.

On the same morning that we found that the back porch door wouldn't shut properly (To the delight of our pit bull, Brian) it appeared that the driver's side door of my car wouldn't close either. Something inexplicable had happened to ensure the locking mechanism was useless and the door swung open of its own accord. It groaned on its hinge and made an awful thud of denial when you tried to shut it closed. We didn't live on a bus route, and the old man had sold his car a few years back based on the observation that he didn't really need to go anywhere. Sure didn't he have me to drop him where he needed going? It had just turned 8 o'clock and I needed to be in the office bang in the middle of town by 9. I had considered cable-tying the door shut as a makeshift fix, but the old man insisted on a more outlandish solution. The last time I'd denied one of his inventions I'd come home to all the furniture in my room glued to the ceiling and so I didn't want to test his madness again.

He led me to his garage, a kip of a hole that depended on a single naked lightbulb for light. The small square room was chaos. There were dismantled car engines and tyres and lawn-mover parts scattered all over the floor. On the wooden worktop there were various tools, some of which I had never seen and others that were hammers and spanners. There were shelves with broken lamps and toasters and radio parts. There were bullets and dismembered manikins and several ovens. There was even a functioning toilet in the corner. The old man avoided his mess and led me to the back of the garage where there was an office chair. He pointed at it with the pride of 3 year-old having used the big boy toilet for the first time. He smiled, before clearing his throat and spitting the green liquid that had been blocking it into a used handkerchief that he kept in his sleeve.

"Take this to work, boy." He sat into it and spun around. There was a joystick on the left armrest that I hadn't spotted and some sort of lever on the right one. He stopped his spinning motion with his feet and pressed on the lever ever so slightly which caused the chair to list forward and create a subtle whizzing sound.

"You put a motor on an office chair? You're one daft aul' man."

"I did and you'll be happy I did. There's three lawn mower motors on this thing. Tops out at about 70 kilometres per hour. This will whip you into town not a badge. You can weave in and out of traffic and all. There's a seatbelt too because I knew you'd be soft about it. You're hardly gonna pay for a taxi to work so just use this and stop cribbing." He stood and pushed the chair in my direction. It was stopped by my knee. I certainly would have paid for a taxi but the fear of this frenzied old man made the chair the more appetising of my choices.

"I made it so the chair won't spin while you're moving so you can keep your eyes on the road. Take her handy and you'll be fine, honest to God." He hocked another glugger, this time spitting it openly onto the floor. The creamy green colour reminded me of the walls in the kitchen.

"You've lost it altogether, lad." I sat into the chair and pulled the seatbelt around me. Somehow the old man had got his hands on an old seatbelt from an airplane cockpit which he had now amalgamated with his needless invention. Below the joystick on the left arm there was a speedometer as well as a small but useful GPS. He was daft, but he'd thought of pretty much everything.

"OK, relax. If I agree to take this thing to work, you have got to get my car sorted by the time I get home. Deal?" He stared back at me like I was a 3 month-old who'd just gotten sick all over him

"Well, of course, it'll be fixed you numpty, that's what I do. I fix things. Sure I fixed that office chair and made it ten times better. Your car won't be any different." That answer only worked to make me even more concerned for the well-being of my loyal Volkswagen. He began rummaging through a nearby box labelled 'Sticky Things' and I decided not to ask any question for fear of the answer. I swivelled the chair around to face the open garage door and gazed out into the crisp morning. It was now 8:25 and the sun was truly on its way to its throne up above. The frozen dew that was painted across the grass in the front garden had begun to thaw, and you knew you'd have wet socks if you stood in it long enough. I leaned lightly on the lever in my right hand and the office chair began to rumble forward. Before leaving the driveway, I allowed myself a few moments to get used to the controls. Once I had familiarised myself with how to stop, I took a deep breath and made my way to the road.

From my house on Bellevue Drive in Grange, it wasn't the furthest drive to Lavitt's Quay in town. Once I reached the city centre I could take the chair off road anyway and walk it to the office. The roads were already extremely busy and the smell of diesel was nauseating as I pulled up behind a car trying to pull out onto the Grange Road. I could see the driver double-taking when she saw me before beginning to shake her head. It took me a moment to realise she was openly laughing at me and to be honest, I completely got it. It was also in that same moment that I realised the old man had neglected to give me a helmet and I cursed myself for putting my life in the hands of an explicitly insane elderly gowleen of man. He'd spent far too many summers inhaling the fumes off the bogs up beyond Tipp and the madness had truly settled in him now. I made a mental note to have him sectioned if I survived my day, before pulling out onto a very loud Grange Road.

When the old man said the chair topped out at 70 kilometres an hour he had been blaggarding entirely; it was much faster. The acceleration speed of the chair was so fast that I needed to lean forward in order to not topple over backwards to my likely death. It was equal parts exhilarating and terrifying. After a few brief minutes, I had become a near-expert and soon I was weaving in and out of idle traffic on a superbly agile reclineable office chair. Passers-by and car passengers alike began to snap pictures of me as I passed and who could blame them. I must have looked the proper eejit gliding down the Frankfield Road at speed on a swivel chair.

The nerves I felt coming into the Kinsale Road Roundabout were justified I feel. After all, the place is an obstacle course within the confined safety of a half-tonne car, let alone out in the open without a helmet on a chair made for sitting at a desk. Already, a local radio station had gotten wind of my journey, as one of their branded traffic cars was now tailing me, presumably to report my movements back to the presenters, and to any driver who might be within my general vicinity. My descent onto the intersection was bumpy and uncertain. There were cars everywhere, which was to be expected in the epicentre of the morning rush hour. I rumbled along the inside lane which became the outside lane as I, at one with the traffic, curved onto the roundabout. Several aggressive horn blasts let me know that other commuters were unsatisfied with my choice of transport. One especially disgruntled punter donning a two-piece suit and some smart spectacles, leaned out of his Corolla and began hurtling every name under the sun in my direction.

I left the Kinsale Road Junction with very little drama and felt more relaxed as I shot down the Souhtlink Road towards the city centre. My approach must have been well documented on the radio because curious on-lookers had gathered on the flyover by Turner's Cross to observe my advance. Although the wind was loud in my ear, I faintly made out the applause and shouts from above as I passed below, which caused an unmistakably cheeky grin to sprawl across my face. The presence of uninvited flies soon put an end to that.

I continued on my journey to town. Soon I was where the Sountlink met Eglinton Street. More notably, Anglesea Street Garda Station loomed up on my left. The Gardaí must have gotten wind of my blatantly illegal commute, as they now formed a road blockade, preventing my progress down a quiet Eglington Street, which would have brought me up around by the City Hall and well on my way to my final destination. The bright green jackets taunted as I grew closer. I could see the smirks and giggles spreading through the flock of Gards. No doubt they thought me a tall fool coming into the city on the wheels of a spinny-chair. With no other options available, I whipped into the left-hand lane, much to the dismay of a young lady driving a Yaris. I pulled back on the lever in my left hand, which caused whatever braking system the old man had installed to screech as I rocketed left down Old Station Road. The lights were in my favour at the junction and I kept moving toward Union Quay via Copley Street. Here, I mounted the curb, shouting at students on their way to the College of Com to get out of my way on Trinity Bridge. I could now hear the sirens in the not so far off distance as I meandered into the less public side streets between Fr Mathew's Quay and the South Mall. The motor on the chair now struggled to keep at walking speed and I knew my evasive manoeuvre at Eglinton Street had all but buckled it. I dismounted the chair just before I reached South Mall, pushing it from behind as I turned left up toward Grand Parade. A squad car zoomed past me with its blue lights flashing accusingly but neither Garda paid me any notice. They were looking for a deranged man driving an office chair up and down the roads, not an average Joe wheeling a chair up on the footpath.

The walk through Paul's Street to the quiet office on Lavitt's Quay was uneventful. It was almost 9 o'clock and most people had apparently already made it to their work places. Nevertheless, the open area outside Tesco was jammed up as always with goth kids and buskers and shoppers. A man with an office chair slipped through unnoticed quite easily. I peeled down the side alley that led to Lavitt's Quay and made my way into reception. I could hear the security guard making coffee in the side room; a room he didn't emerge from before the elevator arrived to bring me to my department on the third floor. The floor was unusually quiet, which I was grateful for as I wheeled a dodgy office chair to my desk. I sat down and logged in. There wasn't one other team member at their desk, yet. The clock on my screen told me it was 8:51 so it was still early yet I reckoned. I didn't piece it together until I went to the coffee dock to refill my water bottle an hour later. As the bottle filled, I flicked through my phone and saw that it was Saturday and that I didn't have to be at work at all. I dragged my feet back to the elevator and left the office without the chair to get a taxi home.

Roses are red
Lilies are white
Backstreet's back
Alright.

The Mayonnaise Overdose
(Inspired by True Events)

You'd probably describe Chef as a character. You'd be chatting about him and then you'd say, "Christ, he's some character." That's what you'd say and you'd be dead right. He was a Garda. That's a police officer for those of you that don't know. Anyone who knows him understands how funny that is because he's a pure messer. Pure gobshite that nobody has a bad word about. You couldn't stick a lick of fowl behaviour to the man. He sucks down Guinness or any stout like a new-born calf at the tit. He'd present himself with a fade fresher than the baker's loaf anytime you might meet him. He's definitely good at this job but I'd often wonder why he's a Garda based on the fact that he's lunatic. The man always had some bizarre story falling out of his mouth, and he told each one with wild conviction and eye contact. No matter how outlandish the tale, you'd want to believe him. That's why I believed him when he told me he OD'd on mayo.

I know what you're thinking; it's not possible to overdose on mayonnaise and I'd be inclined to agree with you. That's exactly what I said to him when he told me first too.

"I did, boy", was his effortless insistence. There is no scientific reason as to why one might overdose on mayo. That being said, it was quite naïve of me to assume this was a scientific matter. A spiritual essence followed the man whether he knew it or not. I'd the feeling his bloodline stretched back as far as Celtic druid baieens performing sketchy pagan malarkey up the high hills in the fog. You'd catch the sparkle of some mad magic in the glint of his eye for just a whisper every so often.

There is some contextual information that you'd need to know before perhaps believing what Chef has claimed to have actually happened. See, Chef had a proclivity for mayonnaise. He couldn't get enough of the stuff. Now, I myself enjoy mayo as much as the next person, but Chef seemed to have some spiritual connection with the egg-based condiment. He put the tangy sauce on every meal, whether it was regarded as something one does or not. It was almost impressive how far he'd go to add mayo to whatever he could. So, to me, if there was anyone on this humble planet that could have overdosed on mayonnaise, it would be this man.

I'll tell it like he told it. It was himself, his mother, and one of the lads in the car. Having come from some match or a training session out the Tower Boreen, they decided they'd take a detour to Douglas in Cork to the almost sacred KCs Sons & Sons chipper; an establishment held to such a high regard in the Greater Cork Area that it is seen as near blasphemy to talk poorly of the place. It wouldn't be uncommon for the line to be a good 20 metres long out the door, The rain might be pelting down with the anger of a feral grandmother and you'd still have punters waiting to get a taste of the much coveted food of the dinky establishment. If the Big Mac is the foundation on which McDonald's is built, then the King Creole is the staple of KCs. It's a simple pitta with chicken, chips, lettuce and a heap of mayo for good measure. Trust me when I tell you it is one of the rare foods that'd bring you closer to God if you're into that sort of thing.

Off they went to KCs anyway. They parked the car across the road in the petrol station which has served as the unofficial carpark for KCs since the dawn of time. Chef didn't mention the length of the queue in his telling, but we'll assume it was long and we'll assume it was raining too for dramatic effect. Chef waited the long wait as the rain battered down upon him from the brooding sky above. In these moments, I often wondered if he knew what was about to unfold. Did Chef know that he was on the brink of a mayonnaise overdose? That his blood would become so saturated with mayo that if he were to cut himself the blood would be a pinky-white colour rather than a deep red? It's almost impossible to say. Drenched to the bone, he queued until he had reached the point of order.

"Next!"

"Howsagoin? Can I get 2 creoles please, extra may in both as well? Nice one, lad."

And that was it. His fate sealed, Chef remained in the queue until his food was ready. His mother and friend both ordered behind him, but those details aren't important to this tale.

I imagine the brown paper that cradled the creoles got wet on the short walk to the car; both from the rain and from the grease seeping out from within. Chef was as ravenous as a young bull elephant having traversed the African plains, and so there was no messing around once he had sat himself into the passenger's seat of the cold car. His mother and friend decided they would wait until they got home to enjoy their meal. That wasn't an option for Chef. He tore into the first creole, barely giving himself a moment to undo the wrapping, and you can be sure he swallowed some paper in that initial sitting. The first of his creoles was gone before they had even gotten up the haphazard ramp that took you from Tesco in Douglas to the Southlink dual carriageway heading westbound toward Ballincollig. He had inhaled the thing, and already his gaze had fallen upon the second creole, his eyes already glazing over from the effects of the heavy-hitter.

Chef stared at the creole. The creole stared back, taunting him. They had just passed the Kinsale Road Roundabout. Chef took a deep breath, picked up the chicken pitta and took his first bite. The chicken was hot and the mayo seemed to gush from the pitta at a ferocious velocity. The car now zipped along the far side of the flyover. The roads were quiet and the streetlights caused the stretch to resemble a runway, a runway that Chef would soon take-off from. Chef took his second bite. There was no chicken; just lettuce and chips and an ocean of mayo. This bite was all Chef's body could take and it wreaked havoc. At tipping point, his blood-mayo level now critical, Chef's body began to malfunction instantly. There were no more groans of pleasure. The creole fell from Chef's hand onto the floor of the car with a squelch. Not even passed Togher yet, Chef had lost consciousness entirely. His head tilted back with the apple of his throat protruding from his neck in a point. His arms were limp and he was unresponsive to the shrieks of his dear mother. Now, when he tells it, Chef puts this down to the high concentration of mayonnaise in his blood. I'm not sure about the scientific consensus on that, but I do trust the man.

His mother and friend began to panic, noticing almost instantly that the young Garda had passed out quite out of nowhere. They shook him and slapped him and shouted and cursed but nothing was working. They were passed Wilton now. His friend decided that they should swing back toward the CUH, a nearby hospital in Bishopstown, because there was clearly something wrong with Chef.

Just as his mother indicated to take the Curraheen exit, Chef stirred in his seat. He began convulsing violently which stopped as quickly as it started. The car fell silent, both mother and friend holding their breath in terrified anticipation. Suddenly, a now wide awake Chef bellowed from his stomach.

"MAYONNAISSSSSEEE!"

He took a deep suck from a water bottle that had been rolling around by his feet before he scooped the barely eaten creole from the floor and began, once more, to inhale its contents. His mother was still driving, still

43

staring at Chef with her jaw almost on the floor. His friend was on his side in the back seat, pulsating in a fit of inconsolable laughter. Chef had passed out but it hadn't broken his stride whatsoever and soon enough he had finished the creole entirely, and had requested to turn back for more. The response to this was a good clip around the ear from his mother, and they carried on towards Ballincollig and into the growing fog beyond. And you can be sure the twinge of druid madness was fresh in the white of his eye that night.

The worst thing about good friends
is that you feel like shit after they've gone home.

Rave Baby

A whirling cocktail of vodka, hash, and vomit creates the very distinct aroma that accompanies the nightlife of Ireland's fairest city. The sweetness, the bitterness and the sour; mixed well into the cacophony that characterises debauchery. Once the clock strikes 11:30 on a Friday evening, the city changes. The veneer of polite sophistication peels away to reveal the primal urges beneath; sex and drugs and lack of forethought. In the summertime, alcohol evaporates off of the skin of red-cheeked rascals like giddy steam. There's a charm to the city's streets as groups of horny youths prowl to find promising establishments. The brown smell of tobacco on fingertips and lips is unmistakable. The confusing metallic taste that only comes from shifting a social smoker lingers in the mouth until it is chased away by brutal shots of tequila and Sambuca.

As the evening drives on, the chatter of lads coming in from the jacks loudens and the influences of Columbian powders become as clear as the gin and tonics that the rugby lads are lashing down in the dark corners of cocktail bars. The night becomes later still, jaws begin to swing wide and low, in tune with the rhythmic tempo of the day's hottest house tracks bumping from the speakers, and pupils widen enough to be able to see the face of God herself. At a certain hour, the comforting sounds of pop and rap music give way to heavy and industrial techno as the late-night rave of Pygmalion begins, and it is here where the true nature of Dublin nightlife can be witnessed if you know what you're doing.

Maura, Chloe and Alannah floated in from the street not long after 11. The summer's air was warm and the fumes of diesel engines were whispering still along William Street South. A balmy grease caused foreheads to shine in with a Dublandish effervescence. There was a buzz about the place, but nothing unmanageable. Away from the chaos of Harcourt Street, the late bar drew a certain type of clientele, one that had no interest in the mayhem provided by Copper Face Jacks.

3 Gin and tonics please. The big glasses now, thanks. Maura had the first round, knowing she wouldn't have to put her hand in the purse for another while. Being out at a grand time on a Friday was ideal. The hangover would come in the morning certainly, but at least there'd be another night of the weekend to deal with it before it was back into the office on Monday. All three worked in the same place doing highbrow consultancy work for one of the biggest banks in the Irish economy. Plenty of money going in there to make up for the pathetic misogyny of the small-pricked big shots. Alannah and Chloe had both come from the same college course into the firm. Maura had been there for a year before

they arrived but they all three had clicked almost instantly. Nevertheless, the girls looked to Maura to take the lead, a role she had no issue with assuming.

Maura wasn't really into house music, never really saw the appeal. Too much unce-unce and not enough words, get me? So when Alannah and Chloe invited her to this DJ that was on, she didn't really have an interest but said she'd go anyway. Sometimes knowing you didn't miss anything is reason enough to do something, whether it's good night or a bad one. Plus, it gave the girls a good excuse to get absolutely loaded and who knows what else.

The three friends clinked a toast in anticipation of the night ahead. Chloe and Alannah chatted excitedly about how much of a lasher this DJ was, and the bar churned on in the background. It was busy enough that you might have to wait a few minutes at the bar, but there was plenty of room to move around. Maura announced that she needed the toilet and the other two reckoned they could do the same. The lad behind the bar said he'd watch their jackets and since the toilet was only a few steps away they figured that'd be alright and headed in.

The toilets were quiet. There were six cubicles, one of which was currently occupied, and by the sound of it, there was more than one person in it. Maura reached the sinks. Making eye contact with Alannah through the mirror, she spun around, the mischief dancing on her face. Right ladies, I don't need a piss at all but I wanted to give ye these before we drive it on. As she spoke she pulled out a tiny zip-lock bag that had 5 little green pills in it. Brian gave them to me. He said they're brand new in from Denmark or Brussels or something and they're meant to be unreal. Like proper heavy. Since we're gonna be at a rave, we may as well rave sure. Alannah casually took one of the pills from Maura and slipped it into the pocket of her jeans. Chloe's brow wrinkled for a split second before reaching to take hers. Maura was too quick on the uptake though and retracted her hand. You don't have to if you don't want to, Chlo. No pressure, like. Maura smiled. It was too late for reassurance. The wheels of peer pressure had already begun to turn. Ah stop now, of course, I want to. Chloe grabbed the pill and squirmed as she decided where to conceal it, eventually deciding the left pocket of her own jeans was the most suitable place. She tapped the pocket, assuring the safe storage of the potent little tablet. Lovely stuff, ladies. Maura clasped her hands together, tilting her chin lightly with a devious smile. Whose round is it?

As the clock sauntered past the twelfth hour, the bar was much busier now than when the trio had arrived. The volume of the music rose relative to the hum of the ever-growing crowd of thirsty bingers. There were some gym-rat boys trying to crack onto a group of selfie demons at the far end of the bar, who were acting uninterested but weren't leaving all the same. Beyond the bar to the left, a door led to another open room. Here there was nothing beside a raised platform that held the DJ's decks and speakers against the far wall. This room was where the real night was set to begin, at around 12:30. Alannah had arrived back to the table now occupied by the trio, with a trifecta of a dark and thick alcohol, as well as 2 cans of Red Bull. Sure I said we may as well drive it on. The end of her sentence lifted, almost as if it were a question, but it was really a result of her being raised far below the border of Leinster. Maura's eyes sparkled with anticipation. Fantastic idea, Al. She reached inside the breast pocket of her shirt as she spoke, and revealed the small green pill from before. I'm gonna take mine now, so I come up when the gig starts. Before either of the other two could protest, the pill disappeared along with the Jaeger bomb Alannah had bought for her. Maura slammed the glass down on the table top and giggled her approval.

At 20 past, more of the crowd made for the back room, trying to get a good spot for the gig. Maura led the girls, pushing her way through a crowd of drunk boys to get to the door. Chloe and Alannah held back to get more drinks. Maura melted into the dark room beyond the bar, as Chloe ordered some vodka whites. Looking around, she produced the green pill from her jeans and broke it in half. She pointed one half at Alannah. Take this there, I don't want to take a full one at all. Her hand tremored slightly as Alannah slowly took the halved pill without breaking eye contact. Maura'll be ragin' now if she knows this. Don't tell her so, Jesus Christ. Chloe hoped she hadn't been too harsh and paid for the round. Chloe asked the bar tender for an additional glass of water and washed down her half pill it. She hoped that whatever the green tab caused to happen wouldn't scare her. She took a deep breath and tightened her grip on the glass to try and stop herself from shaking.

Inside the room, the gig had already begun. It was dark, the only lights being the very dimmed overhead ones. The methodical thump-thump of the bass vibrated through the floor and up into Maura's chest. The hairs on the back of her neck began to dance in rhythm with the drumline. She couldn't say whether the drugs had taken effect yet, but she was certain that she was enjoying this type of music far more than she usually would have. The uniformity, the predictability of it, had all somehow become more appealing and impressive. She wavered slowly on the spot from left to right as she began to connect more and more with the enchanting music. Her eyes brightened up as she saw the 2 girls coming towards her and she realised she had missed them. Chloe handed her a drink and she hugged her in gratitude. Have yous taken yours yet? She screamed over the music into Chloe's right ear. Chloe nodded back as she pulled back from the hug and gave an awkward thumbs up to confirm. Maura smiled and began to waver more intensely, putting her weight into her heels and letting gravity aid her movement.

While the song came to its climactic drop, the full brunt of the little green pill hit Maura with all the might of the pantheon of Greek gods. As the tempo of the deep house elevated before quickly plummeting into a disorientated mixture of sounds, Maura's entire being mirrored it. She felt the place where her mind was at the front of her brain begin to rise, as if it was being pulled from the top of her skull by some euphoria inducing hand. Her pupils widened, almost touching the edges of her irises, making every sliver of light in the dim room glow with intensity. There was a fizzing feel to the air around her, and her skin tingled as she continued to waver with the rhythm of the song. Her legs felt as though they were at one with the treble of the genre house, and Maura knew she couldn't have been more at one with the world around her.

Would you look at that eejit? Alannah nodded toward Maura from her position against the wall. Maura hadn't even noticed them edge away from the busy dancefloor. Christ Al, are we sure she only took one? Maura's legs were vibrating and jolting erratically, completely out of time with the slow tempo of the building track. Her eyes were peeled wide open, and her mouth was in such an open grin that you could see her gums above her bottom lip. She looked like a crazed, dancing clown, who seemed to have no apparent control of her arms, as they flailed about wildly. People had started to give her a weary berth, as she flailed about, her open palms a constant threat. Ah Alannah, we'll have to sort her out. Are we gonna be fucked now as well? Chloe looked into her drink and cursed herself for giving in to Maura. Without replying, Alannah marched over to where Maura was causing wreck and touched her elbow. Maura's smile somehow intensified when she recognised her friend. This is unreal isn't it? She pulled Alannah in aggressively for a hug. Her jaw was going ninety from side to side. We're going to the toilet there if you want to come? Alannah shouted over the loud bass. Maura nodded violently and kissed her teeth as she realised how dry her mouth had become. Alannah took her hand and led her the short distance to the door to the main bar where Chloe was already waiting with a worried look on her face. Maura rushed her and wrapped her arms around the neck of the smaller girl with affection. Aren't you having the best time, Chlo? Before Chloe could answer, Maura doubled over suddenly and let out a long, painful groan. She clutched at her stomach and torso in confused agony before collapsing to her knees with another loud roar. With the music being so loud, and most of the attendees also intoxicated, nobody had even noticed the girl fall to the floor. Alannah and Chloe exchanged worried glances before each grabbing Maura by an arm and walking her the short distance to the toilets behind them.

Maura collapsed onto the toilet seat like the ice falling off the melting caps into cold ocean water below. She searched the eyes of her friends for answers but all that glared back was a great deal of terror. Her midsection convulsed again, more painfully than it had done so far. She squirmed on the seat and feared the worst. Chloe ran from the cubicle at a pace and began throwing up sporadically in the next cubicle over. Alannah helped Maura with her jeans before leaving and closing the door behind her. Whatever was about to come out of her was not something Alannah fancied seeing.

It wasn't long before the guttural roars could be heard outside, from the hushed bar that proceeded the venue centre. One of the bar staff rushed in, a sweaty red-haired Jimbo from out beyond Westmeath gathered himself as he found himself face-to-face with a scared-looking Alannah. What in the name of God is going on in here? I dunno, man. She took a pill. Sure didn't we all. Hasn't everyone here taken something? Anyway, she came up like Drake back in 2009 and all of sudden she's dying in agony. Sure listen, lad, it's fucked. The other one then inside the other toilet puking up her ring. Alannah nodded in the direction of Chloe's cubicle. Ring an ambulance, will you? She doesn't sound right. The barman took out his phone and dialled. No sooner had he put the phone to his ear, the restroom fell silent. Maura's heavy breathing could be heard. This was followed by a very loud splash, as something massive hit the water of the inside of a toilet. There was a brief pause before even more intense screaming and some hair-raising scuttling. These screams weren't from pain, though, these screams had the rattle of fear in them. Something then hit the floor with an unsettling wet flop.

Alannah lunged for the door and swung it open towards her. Maura was passed out on the toilet. She was breathing heavily and her shirt was drenched with sweat mixed with the crimson of fresh blood. But that wasn't what had captured Alannah's attention, causing her to freeze in place. It wasn't what sent the young barman running from the women's toilets. Standing between Alannah and Maura in the threshold of the doorway was the largest baby she'd ever seen. Around a foot and a half tall, its dark hair drenched, its veins protruding from its limbs, chest and neck. Somehow born with the muscle density to stand upright, it was heaving on the spot, as if it were about to dart off at any second. Its mouth splayed in a feral hiss like that of a defensive mountain cat. Yet, it stayed there, pulsating, staring directly into Alannah's soul with its jaw going absolutely 90 from side to side. The wide grimace and the furrowed brows created a menacing, manic effect. The gargantuan infant stood its ground to protect its mother at whatever cost, and Alannah turned on her heel and sprinted for the door with the fear of God hammering in her ears.

I often wondered why
people looked for attention online.
Until I realised
I do the exact same thing when I complain about it
on Twitter.

Fish Tank Lamentations

That damned glass is freezing. I always forget how bloody cold it is. Not cold enough for my lips to get stuck, mind you, but cold enough to tickle my whiskers. That's a metaphor, of course, I don't have whiskers. Or do I? I've not seen my reflection in a long time. I simply do not get it though. The water is fierce warm but the stupid glass is Baltic. I forget every time. Sure I'd only be going over to it to have a look at what's going on in the room. The cat jumped off of that old armchair with such a panic that I knew someone was home. Who was it that was home? I haven't a clue. None of them look familiar nor different to one another. They just lumber around the room like big eejits or sit on that long armchair for ages. I can never really say whether they've been gone for a long time or a short time. I just know that one day I was out there strolling around and the next I was in here trying to kiss cold glass, I think. I don't wanna say that's definitely what happened but it could potentially definitely be what happened.

I'm quite ready to get back to work now, though. I had to take a bit of a break for stress management. At least that's what I was told it was for. I was a professor down in the college teaching English Lit. Very cushy hours. I'd love to get back to doing it but every time I get ready to make the phone call I remember I can't because I'm a fish. And then I forget what I was supposed to be doing the same way these eejits walk through the door of the living room and forget why they came in in the first place. The glass always entices me to its icy kiss and that always makes me forget.

I remember finding out my wife was leaving me, though. Well, that's if she was my wife. There was definitely a woman I lived in the same house as who wasn't a huge fan of me. I sort of remember her coming in and telling me she wanted a divorce when I was sitting down. I don't remember feeling much. I'm not sure if I even responded to her. She was talking loudly for ages anyway and then she left and a few days later she came back and made the rooms feel emptier and left again and I hadn't seen much of her since. Some days I decide I should go out and try and talk to her and figure out what happened, but nearly every time that happens I remember that I don't have legs and can't breathe outside the water. The other times I don't even remember to remember and I find myself drawn to the clear euphoria of that devious glass.

Now I know for certain I had a little daughter. I can even remember her name; it was Molly. She's the only thing I haven't forgotten. I remember how her hair curled slightly at the ends, like flowers turning towards the sun. I remember her laugher, how it sounded like a fresh water spring gurgling on a Summer's afternoon. I remember how her eyes sparkled when she was over-come with the magic of curiosity. Molly had brought meaning to the chaos of my life. Out of the darkness had come this lovely, innocent light and I had never loved something so much or so purely. Molly was the only thing that still made sense, ringing through the confusion and the blur.

The water was particularly warm just then. The glass, of course, still freezing. The cat was still moping around. I remember a time when she used to try and paw her way into my water and try and take me but her arm was too short and I'm actually quite the nippy swimmer. I used to be quite fast on my feet too. I remember I used to race Molly when I had my legs and I would always win and she would sometimes cry after-wards. When I asked her what was wrong one of the times she said she'd wanted to win. I told her that I was an adult and that I would win for now but if she trained every day and worked hard that she'd beat me one day when she was older. She stopped crying shortly after that and started zooming around the garden like an ex-cited puppy. Full of energy with no direction. I like to think I'd been a good father.

The rest of it is a fog. It feels like a dream that I can only remember when I'm not trying to. I definitely had a wife. We were in love for a time but I don't think I always loved her. She was crying when she left and I just sat there staring into the abyss, into nothingness. I hadn't cared. There was something that had happened between us that had caused us both to stop caring. Mol-ly hadn't been there when her mother left me. Maybe she was at her grandmother's, I can't really say for certain. My wife had screamed and cursed and said it had all been my fault. If I could just remember, instead of losing it to the vagueness of this tank every time.

Every day the water feels like I've known it forever, yet feels brand new at the same time. The way it envelopes me entirely with its invisible grip. It has a thickness to it, suspending me far above the bottom of the tank. It's odd, though, once you live in water you never worry about whether you're drinking enough of it, your body just absorbs it. Every morning when I wake, I panic briefly as I realise I'm underwater and think I'll drown. But then I breathe and remember and wonder if all fish wake up feeling the same way. I wonder if all fish used to be people and woke up one day to find that they were fish and had to try and figure it out. I wonder about all of that until I forget and find the glass again and curse myself for being so weak when I realize that the transparent sand seduced me once again.

My wife had definitely been crying when she was leaving, and she was jabbing her long index finger into my chest and it hurt and I didn't even stand up to see her off. I just sat there and gazed onwards. I remember, yes, that she came back! And she was crying even more now and was apologising and saying it wasn't fair to blame me for what happened because I was hurting too. And I still gazed onward and then she took my chair, the one I was sat on and turned it. And I was facing her and the chair was moving so freely still and then she walked behind me and I couldn't see her anymore and then I started moving forward, still in my chair, towards the door that led from the kitchen to the living room. It dawned on me then that I wasn't being a rude prick or not talking or standing up. I remember now I couldn't do any of those things because I was paralysed and she was pushing me on a chair with wheels and I couldn't do much of anything for myself.

The memory hit me like a flood of cold water from above and although you couldn't tell I was crying because I'm a fish, I definitely knew I was crying because that's how it felt. Yet I still couldn't remember exactly why. The memory of the wheelchair and the guilt and the pain had entered my body and I could feel it now but I still could not remember why I felt that way. And then it subsided as quickly as it had begun and I swam along and forgot once more about it all.

A few weeks rolled by. Or maybe it was a few hours or months. You can never tell in here. The faceless people had come in and out and in and out. They dropped food in and I lost myself against the glass more often than I can remember and I had the odd moment of lucid memory of being in a suit and there being loads of people and only really seeing their faces when they bent down to look me in the eye to tell me they were sorry whilst they tried to shake my dead hands. But then I'd flip right back to swimming and thinking about the glass and the scary water all around.

Then one morning I was waking suddenly and I was drowning and I wasn't in the water. I was gasping in the tight air that now seemed alien and I could feel the slime drying away from my skin and my body flapped madly of its own accord in an attempt to survive. I could feel a fabric around me and my vision was blurring fast and I couldn't breathe at all and things were going very dark. The burning pressure on my chest expanded until it felt like it would burst and then there was no more floundering or breathing and my vision all but went. And as I lay there drowning in the light air, I could remember the headlights coming towards me and the noise and panic and the tiny small wooden box as it went down below. And I could remember Molly's lovely laugh trickling from her like water as I slipped into the big nothing.

At this stage, you've read enough that you may as well finish it out.

Sunk Cost Effect, baby

Late Night Petrol-Pump

Smells of lovely diesel drew me in as I refilled my filthy Volkswagen with the colourless liquid. The thought always crossed my mind that I was pouring what was essentially dead dinosaur juice into a metal container, which in turn allowed me to move around more easily. It was during these moments, as the fumes of the intoxicating danced in my nostrils, that I thought about how strange life was. We were fundamentally just very intelligent apes, weren't we? Actually no, intelligence isn't what separated us. We were very arrogant apes, consumed by a feeling of superiority. The fact that we had gotten to a stage where I could be standing at a petrol station at 5 past 11 on a Wednesday evening filling up my car to drive home was unbelievably bizarre when one really put thought into it. I had the means to do a lot of things, but if you told me I had to go out and fend for my own dinner and keep warm and healthy without the help of what we had become, I'd be dead within the week. That's why we were arrogant. We're more intelligent in certain aspects, certainly. But I don't know how to effectively live without cheat codes, and that goes for most of us.

I looked around as the diesel meandered slowly through the hose. The station was empty aside from me. It was one of those self-service ones that only takes card. A modern breakthrough for the socially anxious. There wasn't even a shop, which was a pity because I was gasping for a drink of water. There were the dregs of a bottle on the floor of the passenger's seat side, so I reached in and drained it to curb the thirst. There was a self-service car washing facility behind me near the fence. Beyond that the train track sprawled, stretching toward town. I was the only person in that quiet station. A video camera glared down at me from the corner of the roof that sheltered the pumps. I looked up and gave a knowing wave. Maybe whoever had the misfortune of being on the other end of the feed would get a laugh from that.

Across the road there was a long, one storey building with some roadside parking outside of it. One half of the building was a shop and the other half was a diner. Pure American looking in the middle of rural Ireland. The area was a popular spot for truck drivers to pull in for the night to sleep, but there were only a couple of deserted Arctic lorries parked up along the side of the road that night. There were a couple of cars parked outside the diner too. By now the condensation had already begun to creep up windscreens, threatening to freeze. Behind the building the land rose into a hill, and the lights from houses dotted the darkness like lanterns.

I turned my attention back to the pump. The diesel continued to guzzle and crackle as it made its way into the undercarriage of my car. Most of us don't even know how cars really work, do we? I know I didn't. Put the ancient liquid in, turn the key, drive away. Completely oblivious to the how of it all. Jesus Christ, this particular pump was unbelievably slow. The counter clicked upwards at a crawl and it felt as though I'd be standing at that pump forever. My patience was wearing thin when there was a distinct bang across the road. I looked across. My eyes took a few seconds to adjust to the darkness. The inside light of one of the parked cars was now on and the silhouette of a woman was standing outside. The hot glow of her lit cigarette illuminated her face softly as she inhaled the addictive tar. Faint bags lined the bottoms of her eyes and her cheek bones protruded from a narrow face. She began to walk towards me. Well, not towards me directly I imagine, that was hardly the case. She began to walk in my general direction, towards the petrol station. I could hear her boots thudding on the concrete above the rumble of the slow pump. I hadn't a notion why she was walking this way but I averted my gaze all the same.

She crossed the boundary line that distinguished between the parking area and the hard shoulder. Now on the tarmac of the road she took another pull from her cigarette. I could smell the smoky whispers of the tobacco. She reached the centre of the road, where the broken line split the lanes. From out of the night, the obnoxious sound of an engine with its silencer removed could be heard only a few hundred meters down the road to my left. It groaned and lurched with aggression. The volume of it, and how quickly it became louder, suggested that the vehicle was travelling at pace. Moments later the faint beams illuminated the road, growing more intense as they focused upon the woman looking up with the cigarette still between her lips. Then there was screeching that was all too late and then there was impact, blood-curdling impact.

The metal of the bonnet moaned painfully as it made contact with the woman's midsection. Like a rag doll, she tumbled over the bonnet with the panic of violence and was thrown hard into the window. The windscreen cracked loudly as her head and arms collided with it and the car swerved into the other lane. As the woman came to the ground with a wrenching permanence, the car squealed, fleeing from the scene like a frightened rodent. The pump had finally finished pumping and the decisive click was followed by a deafening silence. A dark shadow grew slowly from the limp woman in the middle of the quiet road. I wasn't sure what to do so I stood there for a minute longer. The woman still hadn't moved.

I walked towards her. A silent breeze filled the road. The lights that illuminated the petrol station dimly lit the road in a dusky shadow. I could smell the tang of burnt rubber as I approached. Even from the hard shoulder line I could see that her left arm was at a disturbing angle. Her elbow had hyperextended and become caved in so that her arm appeared to bend the other way. A similar, but less severe fracture had happened to her right knee which caused her right foot to bed up towards her torso. The bloody shadow was growing slower now. The woman's grey overcoat was darkened on the back and sides as the life-giving liquid soaked in. She lay there on her back, legs and arms disfigured and ruined. Yet her face was untouched and seemed peaceful somehow. Her eyes were still open, gazing softly into the unknown ceiling of stars that spread out above her. Her mouth was closed in an unhappy smirk. She looked to be around middle-aged, although it was clear that she looked younger than she was.

I blinked in the silence of death. The stars seemed almost melancholy now, twinkling their choreograph in response to tragedy. I gazed up at them and wondered if the woman was somewhere out amongst them now. My brain told me no but my heart wasn't so sure. It made no difference anyway. She was definitely not here.

I closed her eyelids for her. With a gentleness, I reached inside the pocket of the woman's jacket and found her phone which was locked. Her keys were in the other pocket and I decided to use them to open her car. I found her licence in the sun visor on the driver's side. Her name was Allison Tully. She was soon to be 46. She was smiling in her licence picture and I felt that she had been a sweet woman. I put the licence back and closed the door before returning to Allison and making the phone call I probably should have made minutes ago.

I waited until the ambulance came. It didn't take long and the flashing blue lights of the response vehicle made the roadside feel like a crime scene. One of the paramedics brought me under the lights of the filling station and took my statement. I told her everything I had seen although I hadn't been able to get the registration number of the car who'd hit the woman. I told them it was a dark-colored Toyota Corolla. They put her body in the back of the ambulance and whizzed off; the blue lights still flashing without any siren on. I returned to my car and drove the short journey home and that was that.

I was told not to worry about things when I was
younger
and it's been on my mind ever since.

I Just Wanted a Muffin, Man

Fixating on small, seemingly insignificant things, is no good way to deal with an actual issue. Of course, when you fixate on things of this nature, you'd hardly be privy to the knowledge of a more unsettling problem.

Take for example the fact that I'd had an exam that Tuesday afternoon. I hadn't done a lick of study for it, nor had I even gone to a lecture all semester. I'd be better served throwing shapes toward the student bar for a gawk at the Freshers. The lecturer was a wreck head as well, and had a penchant for over promoting himself. So it wasn't too shocking that I was in the Dunnes on Patrick's Street, less than two hours before the exam, freaking out because there were no chocolate muffins left. Not even a one. There were plenty of blueberry ones left, but fuck that. I needed chocolate chip. It was a sort of ritual of mine in a way, to have a moist chocolate muffin before the final exam. You might understand how frustrating a blueberry muffin is when you don't want one, would you? I found myself boiling over due to the presence of countless blueberry muffins. This was a real issue. Forget that exam for the time being. I just wanted a chocolate-chip muffin. Before leaving (without my muffin) I screamed quite loudly at the manager by the till. A lot of people stared at me, they almost seemed alarmed in a way. After that, I left the shop. The security guard walked with me. He told me it was probably better if I didn't come back and shop there, at least for a while. I smiled at him in silence. It wasn't my fault they didn't have the right muffins.

I zipped down past the back of Opera Lane, passed the oversized Boots on the corner to my right, and navigated up through Paul Street. The noise cancelling headphones I owned forced any other people out of awareness beautifully. My exam was at 4 PM in the Maradyke. It was now 3:07. I had plenty of time. I hadn't studied much really, but I did flick through all the lecture slides at the beginning of study month, so at least I had the majority of those in my head. People rarely believe me when it comes up that I have photographic memory, but I don't care so much. I still had it whether they believed me or not. I did my best to not have it come up. Some of my friends like to bring it up to impress people, like it's some sort of cheap parlour trick they can use to earn clout. I've told them on several occasions that the memory I have doesn't work the way they want it, yet they continue to bring it up, asking me to recite ingredients on random drinks and foods. When I fail to do so, they call me a liar, or a bullshitter and that's the end of that. It's as if they think I consciously control my memory. They conveniently forget that none of them have control over their own memory either. It's selective and it's very particular, like evolution, baby. I have photographic memory when it's motivated by learning and pressure. That's it. I couldn't tell you a thing about my childhood, but I could draw a nephron from a kidney to perfection for you if you wanted. I got an A1 in Leaving Cert Biology so I did.

So the exam was gonna be fine. I may not get full marks but I'd get damn near close. I stayed right on Paul's Street and turned up towards the street that TK Max is on. I never bothered to learn the name of it. I was gonna chance the Lidl there next to TK for a muffin. I waited on the escalator as it allowed my descent below ground into the giant, air-conditioned room that made up Lidl. It was quiet. No such thing as a Tuesday afternoon rush. I skimmed down the first aisle to where the bakery section was. Unlike its almost identical competitor, Lidl had freshly baked goods, which made it superior in my eyes. What this Lidl did not have, though, were chocolate muffins. My eyes met the muffin stand to see a bountiful supply of blueberry muffins yet again. The abundance of blueberry muffins juxtaposed by the lack of chocolate chip caused a very large dose of ancient rage to swell inside of me. The type of feral anger I imagine Cu-Chulainn had when he drove that sliothar down the throat of that bastard dog. I didn't even try to control the primal scream that erupted from me. It reverberated around the quiet supermarket quite nicely. I'd been to two shops within the last hour, both of which were outspoken about offering the best in grocery needs, and neither of them could fulfil the simple request of a muffin. I was furious. I retreated to the top of the store and made my way to a teller, empty-handed. In these shops you can't just exit; you have to go through the till. It's a mechanism purposely designed to make you buy something out of conformity and social awkwardness. I shuffled down toward the cashier. The woman at the cashpoint looked up at me, and when I was about 4 feet away I barked at her. Not too loud a bark, about as loud as a mid-sized Retriever. Nevertheless, she seemed quite startled, and pulled back away from me as I came level with her. I barked at her again for good measure before continuing out of the shop. She looked confused, or scared, I wasn't sure. No muffins, once again.

It was 3:16 when I left the Lidl. It had begun to rain lightly so I pulled my hood up over my ears. I wasn't even hungry, but the fact that I couldn't get a muffin had thrown me for coppers. I felt like a failure, and I cursed myself for not being more of a man. A real man could provide things like muffins. Mufasa, from the Lion King, would have definitely gotten some chocolate chip muffins. He was a real man and he wasn't even a man. A cartoon lion was more of a man than I was, and it felt like the whole world knew it.

I began to walk, defeated, towards the Maradyke. I dragged my feet along Maradyke Walk, past Pres, the skate park, and the rest. It wasn't exactly fair, was it? I worked so hard in college, and at everything else. Then, when I ask the universe for a simple gesture in return, it is spitefully denied. Nothing ever went right for me. College was unbelievably boring. Still living with my parents was disappointing, and now I couldn't even get my hands on a simple muffin. Life was tough for me, and nobody even noticed or cared.

I went and sat the exam. People asked me after how it had gone. I told them it went fine and they seemed unpleased about that. I was probably meant to pretend to be unsure. I wasn't unsure. That was my last exam before summer. I went home afterwards, screamed at my mother and slept for 12 hours. My day had been almost unbearable. I woke up with my tongue stuck to the top of my mouth so I reached to the side of my bed and gulped in some cool water that had a metal taste to it.

The exam results were released online on the 21st of June that year. I logged on three hours after the release. The system is quite slow in the initial half hour or so when everyone else is eagerly checking. I hadn't been worried. I flipped through and almost hit the screen when I saw that I had failed that last exam by 3 percentiles. I also hadn't got as high as I thought I did in anything else. Those pricks had to have marked me down. There was no way I would have scored so low. I only failed the last exam because the world had failed to deliver me a muffin. None of these results reflected me. Those pathetic lecturers had it out for me. They knew how much smarter I was than everyone. I quickly tweeted *"Life is toughest for those who can handle it"* from my iPhone X. My mom got it for me after I'd finished my exams but I'd have preferred a Samsung.

Drink more water, seriously.

Millennial Behaviour Dissociation

Mel and Jordan had been going out almost two years when Jordan broke it off. A quick job. He did it by text from the comfort of his couch at home. He'd paused the PlayStation, typed out his brief explanation and sent it off. Two ticks in the lower right-hand corner was all he needed to un-pause his game and continue. Jordan had never really cared. He didn't have the ability to truly care, but it was a handy number. Mel was great, and lovely, and smart, and a belter. She was a catch for sure. Jordan knew that but he couldn't bring himself to actually give a shit. It was all so on the surface for him. She was a part of his life but she could easily not have been, and now she wasn't. He wouldn't give much more thought to it than he already had. His emotional land-scape remained undisturbed. Or perhaps it remained completely disturbed? That's probably more appropri-ate. Later that afternoon, Jordan re-downloaded Tinder and began the process again. The only emotions he felt were loneliness and anger for the next few weeks, and sure wasn't that business as usual?

Mel, in contrast, was completely heartbroken. The message came in early Saturday morning, and her soul lit up when she saw Jordan's name pop up on her screen. Her lovely boy. That glow quickly ousted, and her stomach hurtled to the floor as she read the very apathetically written message. The tears began falling well before she had finished her first reading of the brief message. Screen shots were taken and sent to group chats. She tried to ring Jordan to see what was going on, several times, but had no success. The girls ineffectively consoled her and said unhelpful things like how they had never liked Jordan to begin with. Mel's whole life, her reality for the past two years had been shattered by one, lazy WhatsApp message. Mel's heart felt like it had been ripped from her. The sadness collided with her pride and transitioned to blind rage within a matter of hours. She deleted Jordan from every social media channel she had, along with any pictures she had of him on her feeds. She took to Twitter, said something about all men being assholes and denounced them entirely. Mel posted thirst-trap selfies to the Gram with a caption that suggested a similar message to her Twitter. She checked his story every hour or so to see what he was up to. None of that made it any better, but it temporarily distracted her.

Of course, Mel got over Jordan. She realised he was just a narcissistic boy. Her thing from then on was about finding a man. Boys like Jordan wouldn't make the cut anymore, but due to his hurtful actions, not many men would ever hit the mark either. She developed a thicker skin, and refused to take any future rela-

tionship she had too seriously. Mel still dated, and had her fun, but nothing lasted longer than a few weeks before she either called it off, or ghosted the guy entirely. The next 3 boyfriends were cheated on.

It turned out that Jordan had an undiagnosed emotional disorder, sort of. It couldn't really be classed as one considering it affected a majority of men between the ages of 18 and 30. Social media had a major role to play in that. Mel and Jordan belonged to a generation that almost never committed due to a subconscious belief that the grass could always be greener. There was always the potential to come across someone more suitable and so nobody really committed to much. This was juxtaposed with the pressure to be in a relationship. Very few people were able to commit, but nobody wanted to be single. This led to an influx of superficial, surface relationships. Ones that were good for Instagramming, and for regular sex, but where no meaningful emotional connection actually existed.

Men such as Jordan begin to believe that there is something wrong with them, and to an extent they're correct. Multiple failed relationships due to an inability to attach emotionally points to an internal fault. So men like Jordan may develop an internalised source of depression due to a lack of emotional availability. This coupled with a cultural taboo on men to express emotions results in an inability to seek out help and support when it is needed. Therefore, many of these types of individuals end up dead by suicide.

On the other hand, women like Mel develop a heightened level of insecurity which may manifest in in-

creased levels of promiscuity and a need for affirmation from strangers. Social media channels facilitate this need which causes the insecurity to become a cycle which is difficult to break if one is not aware. Although this situation may be less likely to lead to suicide, it is possible that it will lead to many women being dead long before they stop living.

Neither of these situations are good. Both are a result of poor emotional maturity and the impact of social media. Both situations can be avoided, with the right education. ·

Peter clicked off of the ad for the intro to psych class available down the community college. That was by far, the strangest pop-up that had ever come up on Porn-Hub, ever. It had not helped with the hangover anxiety either, especially when the description of this Jordan character hit home beyond tolerance. He rolled over in bed and left out a moan that expressed the depth of his struggle. This hangover was truly battering down the walls of his mind, and it wasn't long before he was twitching his way back to sleep, hoping he'd wake up in less pain, whilst also terribly aware of how dehydrated he was.

Peter awoke 47 minutes later, drenched in cold sweat. The day had changed to a murky dusk, leaving his mind confused and wondering where he was. The light from outside the window was faint, leaving the room feeling like it was stuck in its own shadow. For a few fleeting seconds Peter, the beer-bellied 25-year-old, felt free of his hangover. This solace ended as soon as he moved his tongue, revealing the Sahara Desert like conditions within his mouth. He reached for the half-empty bottle of water beside his bed and sucked down some of the contents. By now, the part of the hangover which rendered the individual unable to drink water was over. Thus, the water was glorious, and Peter felt like the Salmon of Knowledge had just entered his bloodstream and possessed him. The water coursed through him, just like the Holy Spirit did to those cripples who were healed on YouTube. The water was good.

Peter slumped back onto his back, satisfied entirely. His hangover was coming to an end, and he promised himself that he'd stay off of the drink for the foreseeable future, and would only have a few if it was an occasion. To make the promise more concrete, Peter flicked his Twitter app open and typed, "*Off the drink now for a while, can't be dealing*", and sent it out into the ether. Nobody liked the tweet, and it was likely that nobody believed it either.

No less than 48 hours had passed since Peter's promise, since his vow on Twitter. Peter woke up with a grinding headache, and the relentless feeling that he was a terrible person. He opened his eyes, still squinting, and could feel the remnants of vodka behind them. The alcohol was still dancing in his eyes. No Garda would have let this man away without breathalysing. Within a few moments, he tasted the horrible sweetness of bile, and vomited on his crotch before he could move himself to the bathroom, which was only across the landing from his room. The black tar of 2AM vodka cokes spluttered onto groin and stomach, and he shouted in agony. He got up, chunks of fresh vomit falling in his wake, and stumbled to the toilet. He vomited painfully for the second time down into the sink, and he could already hear his mother lecturing him. He lumbered into the shower, jocks still on, and washed away as much of his shame as he could, but he knew there was far more shame than one could scrub away in one 5-minute sitting.

It was 8:21AM when he finished in the shower. Work began at 9. He tactically vomited once more for good measure, flushed it away and brushed his teeth before leaving the bathroom. Peter put on some relatively clean slacks and an un-ironed shirt, some funky socks and the brogues he wore the night before, which had speckles of dried-in bile on them. He rushed out the door of the family bungalow and hopped into his dinky Ford Fiesta. The world was still moving without warning, but he turned the ignition and pulled out of the driveway and into the quiet country road. The concrete that stretched out before him gestured at him to speed, and the drink still within his blood told him it wasn't a bad idea.

Peter had been driving for 6 minutes, at a speed of 96 kilometres an hour, when he collided with the railing along the side of the South Link. The car's front driver's side tire clipped the exterior railing, causing the car to spin into the outside lane and flip 4 times before coming to a halt. 2 more cars crashed as a result. Nobody was seriously injured, but Peter was dead before the car flipped for its 3rd time. The ambulance arrived through the tunnel at the Dunkettle interchange and the traffic began to queue along the motorway that snaked its way alongside the river toward Midleton. There were plenty of people late for work that day, and Peter's mother received a phone call no mother is ever ready to get.

The words, 'You're never right the morning after. Don't drink and drive.' Slowly filled the black screen.

"Jesus Christ", Máire breathed out, "Those drink-driving ads are getting completely out of hand, that was like a fucking Tarantino movie". Ciara let out a giggle and then clasped her open hand over her mouth to stop herself.

"Will you mind what you're doing, you'll blow it all away!" Máire barked at Ciara, pointing at the 4 lines of cocaine, that were drawn neatly on the coffee table. The two girls were alone in their house on College Road, only a five-minute walk from campus. It was 11AM and so the rest of their housemates were either still in bed since the night before, or else had actually made it to class. Máire took a tenner from her purse and rolled it effortlessly into a cylinder, and brought it to her left nostril, her snorting nostril. Ciara watched perched on her armchair, gleefully awaiting her own turn. There were empty beer cans and the butts of cigarettes everywhere, but neither girl seemed to take any notice.

"Right Ciara, this is my last time doing coke, it can't be good for us at all." Máire expertly placed the end of her 10 euro-note cylinder at one end of one of the white lines and inhaled a loud snort, which was followed be a stinging grunt and the words, "Fuck me."

No doubt you're wondering why I wasted my time writing this book, huh?

It's a good question that has no answer.

Species Fluid

During the summer months, the island was always at peace with the sky at day break. Where the ice thawed and crept quietly into the grass, a middle-aged penguin trudged in the opposite direction of the glimmering ocean. The water descended in droplets down her rubber-like skin as she waddled towards the town and towards the day ahead. The morning swim had cleared her head, but the stress of the week wouldn't fully diminish. There were 13,000 penguins living on the island; a small fraction of the overall population around the Globe. Still, this particular nugget of land was home to the most divisive social debate on the entire planet. News outlets from every corner of the map had been coming in troves all week to get first word of the parliament's final say on the issue. Today, Amanda Glacier had to deliver the news to the world, news she herself supported. However, she knew that the same news would have repercussions that could cause uproar, discrimination and violence from supporters of both sides of the divide. That day would go down in history forever, and Amanda was feeling the full weight of the news she would soon deliver as she waddled towards Parliament House.

The huge dome that was the central building for the governing body of Penway rose up like the shadow of a great beast. From afar the building looked like an emperor hunched over, but from up close the intricacies of the architecture gave the grand illusion that the entire building was carved from one giant piece of ice. It was an impressive building, one that symbolized penguin pride and power for miles around. The colossal structure, aptly named 'The Emperor's Palace', had once been home to the great leaders of the Emperor penguins down through the centuries. In modern times, it had been upgraded to facilitate the needs of a government with a global impact and a growing population. The furious chatter of penguins in the near capacity main hall of Parliament A could be heard from outside the building. Not just penguins either, as many different species of sea bird had sought the island too. The news that would break that morning wouldn't just affect penguins, but indeed all species of bird. This was colossal. Butterflies fluttered around Amanda's stomach as she entered the odyssey. Her presence was felt immediately. Amanda's descent of the steep steps into the centre of the pit-like amphitheatre brought a hush to the capacity crowd. Not a bird took a breath as Amanda Glacier, the Prime Minister of Penway, waddled her way down the steps and up onto the podium.

The microphone screeched as she approached it, causing her, and many of the birds present to wince in discomfort. Prime Minister Glacier took a sip of water from the glass on the podium, cleared her throat and began to speak.

"Esteemed colleagues, brothers and sisters from around the Globe, welcome to you all. I shall get directly to the point. As you know, the final count of our recent referendum has been tallied and the result deliberated. As is the way with groundbreaking and progressive steps towards tolerance and inclusion, there will be many who oppose this historical result. It is the duty of this government to champion the voice of the people, and that voice screams for a society of conclusion for all walks of life. From January 1st 2035, free and safe trans-species procedures shall be provided to any penguin who identifies as a bird of flight, and also to any bird of flight that identifies as a flightless penguin. Thank you for your patience this morning, and thank you for pioneering an incredibly proud movement."

Prime Minister Glacier stepped off the podium. The room immediately erupted into a medley of celebratory applause and intolerant outrage. The security team was already rushing in to move the Prime Minister safely through a side door which led onto the street and into her private car. Amanda Glacier hunched into the backseat and left out a sigh of relief. The work was far from done. She was still stressed. The fallout from the morning's announcement was going to be huge, and it looked like it would be equal parts positive and negative.

For years, if not decades, there had been an outcry for something to be done for the trans-species birds. These birds, through no fault of their own, had an unwavering and relentless feeling that they had been born within the wrong species. Mostly, this identity crisis revolved around birds that couldn't fly who believed that they were born with the need to fly. Many argued that the idea of a species was in itself a social construct, and that just because you were assigned a species at birth, it didn't mean you had to conform to that species. The trend, and what appeared to be a rise in popularity of trans-speciesim, matched the progressive and liberal culture of the modern world. The announcement of the successful referendum showed the planet that Penway was ready to move forward, and move forward it did.

Unfortunately, although the sentiment was noble and hearts were in the right place, there is only so much a society can do with the technology one has. Trans-species surgeries were given to any birds who wanted them, yes, but of course, these procedures were primarily aesthetic in nature, as science hadn't yet figured out how to give flightless birds the ability to fly. The island nation of Penway began to see an influx of penguins from all countries, as the procedure was not yet available anywhere else. The newly specied birds felt more accepted and more comfortable with themselves, now donning their feathers, which were the universal mark of a bird of flight. Many other types of bird identified as flightless penguins, and so their procedure resulted in feathers being removed, to be replaced with a layer of blubber-skin mesh that was harvested from beached whales and seals.

The end result of these procedures was a society where everyone had the option to feel more comfortable with who they were, and for the most part, the general population accepted these trans-birds with empathy and compassion. However, as it goes with nearly all things, there were some dissenters, who believed the procedures, and indeed the ethos of trans-speciesism was an abomination. Unfortunately, this group appeared to be loud, powerful, and essentially everywhere. Online, individuals ripped into the idea of trans-speciesism, not taking into consideration the feelings or mental state of penguins who identified as a different species of bird. The lack of empathy, and apparently purposeful ignorance, only worked to demonize trans-species birds across the world. Nevertheless, the support for those who were trans-species remained within liberal circles, and the government continued to support and encourage the progressive route forward.

3 years had passed since the historic day in the Palace of the Emperor in Penway. For the most part, people got on with their lives. Penguins and trans-penguins co-existed. Life marched on as usual. Penguins of Penway mainly worked in fishing and seafaring industries, and by 2038 the economy was flourishing.

The rain flurried down in icy spirals as Amanda Glacier made her way to the opening of the new Children's hospital in the north-west of the island, near the business quarter. Flicking through her newsfeed, she came across a video that was trending online. It was an interview on Good Morning Penway, conducted by quite a famous commentator. He appeared on screen, visceral and exasperated. The penguin was slightly overweight and had a posture that appeared confident and comfortable. He was talking about the trans-species ideology, and he wasn't holding back

"It's become ridiculous is what I say. There is no scientific basis for what is happening. The world is simply pandering to the moans of a minority because they have somehow convinced themselves of something that isn't real. I won't stand for it." The smug penguin paused for a moment to gather himself for his next swing.

"In fact, if any penguin can identify as a bird who can fly, why stop there? Now that I think about it, I believe that I'm a human being born into a penguin's body. Yes, I actually identify as a human being and there is nothing anyone can do to say otherwise." The video ended there. It had over a million views already and was steadily growing. The comments section was alive with a mixture of support, outrage, disgust, and anything in between. It was a total shit storm.

By Wednesday of the same week, it was all anyone was talking about, both online and in real life. Most people said they believed it to be deeply insensitive. The group chat comments of many of these same penguins would suggest otherwise. Although the world might have appeared to be inclusive, the support of this view on trans-speciesism would suggest that bigotry still flourished. Nevertheless, before the end of the same week there were petitions everywhere demanding that this broadcaster be thrown off the island for his bigoted views. His social media channels were mobbed by thousands of people, both in support of his views and against them, all making their unoriginal and uninteresting opinions heard.

Amanda Glacier met with a small group of the cabinet to discuss the potential this new drama had for public disorder. It was clear that, although it was unwise to give into the demands of the mob, anarchy would descend on the island of Penway if the government ignored the issue entirely. To add even more fuel to the fire, the penguin who had begun all of this chaos had not remained quiet. Not only had he typed out his words and sent them into the ether to further emphasise his point, he went as far as recording several more videos that echoed the same sentiment; That he identified as a human being and that nobody could tell him otherwise.

The news continued to cover the issue, and the penguin at the centre of all of this continued to become even more infamous, gaining fans and haters in equal proportions. It was now clearer than ever that, although the 3-year-old referendum had gained majority support, there was not a majority support of the trans-species group whatsoever.

After several gruelling weeks of angry citizens, both online and those protesting around the parliament building, Prime Minister Glacier finally got her meeting with the controversial, opinionated penguin. Away from the cameras this penguin was well mannered, amicable and leagues apart from the bravado he had shown online. He was almost shy. Glacier was almost convinced that Michael, her secretary, had gotten the wrong guy for the meeting. However, it didn't take too long to clear up that she had the right penguin. The conversation started with some pleasantries, the usual disclosure concerns and what have you. Whilst Glacier poured coffee over ice, the outspoken penguin got straight down to it.

"With all due respect, Prime Minister, we both know why I'm here. There's civil unrest and you need a solution. I for one, think you should just do it." He leaned back in the chair, his fin-like wings cradling the back of his head, as he smiled smugly.

"Do what exactly, Mr. Morgan?". She didn't look up from the pour.

"Send me away. Cast me from the island. Make an example of me. I don't care what you do. At the end of the day, I don't want to be here as much as the people can't stand the sight of me. I'll join the humans." Glacier looked up, expecting an outburst of laughter. What she found was a glint of sincerity in the eyes of the penguin opposite her. The idea that he could have been serious had never struck her. It hadn't ever struck anyone by the look of things.

"You… want to live with the humans? You'll willingly to leave? To be candid with you, it would wrap up all of this mess and bother neatly for us." She gestured to the empty room.

"I may be a lot of nasty things, but I'm not a liar. I know of penguins who have gone before to live in the human colonies, and I want that. I've never fit in here so maybe I'll fit in there." There was a melancholy to his voice. His eyes had drifted up and to the left as he imagined his new life with the humans.

"Well, Mr. Morgan, if it's what you want, and it's the will of the people, then I don't see why it cannot be. It'll take a few weeks but you have my word that we'll see you through to the human colonies to the north." Glacier stood and reached out her wing to make good on the deal. Mr. Morgan stood and slapped his own wing off of the Prime Minister's, the noise of which smacked loudly around the room.

"Excellent news altogether, and please, call me Piers."

As sure as hash is brown
And as sure as pudding is black
Nothing says death
Like a heart attack.

Jay-Zeus Walks

Harsh sunlight was already hammering the eyelids of Jay as he woke. The thin skin was a hazy red in the sun's presence. Before he opened his eyes, he knew he was outside. The light breeze lapped at his shaved scalp and he could hear the casual chorus of birdsong to his right, which was almost drowned out by a large, unfamiliar noise all around. It was a day that would cause many to sun burn, and Jay's eyes took a minute to adjust. He was lying on the grass with a short blanket wrapped around him. The grass spread out in front of him for about 25 meters, with a concrete pathway that coiled its way around bushes and trees towards a small wall, on top of which sat a fence made of metal columns. There was an opening in the fence for people to exit onto the sidewalk outside, which ran parallel to a wide and busy road. Colossal buildings, bigger than any Jay had ever seen, lined up on the other side of the roadway. Cars raced up and down the road like angry hornets as people went about their day.

Jay observed his surroundings. He had never seen these fast metal carriages before. The noise they made was loud and urgent. They growled like hungry dogs do standing over food. The buildings glaring down on him looked impossibly built, and Jay felt as though they could fall in on him at any moment. Although his surroundings were shocking and unrecognizable, Jay was surprised to feel a deep sense of calm. He felt as though all of this was familiar even though none of it was recognizable.

Looking around, Jay realised he was stark naked, as he lay outstretched on the grass. The small blanket only reached as far down as his belly button, and so the bottom half of his body was on show to the entire world. Several cars emitted loud honks as they passed by, yet Jay did nothing to cover himself up. Instead, he stood up, reached his hands up over his head to stretch out his long, peaky back, and began to meander towards the gap in the fencing. He stopped briefly, after spotting a puddle on the path and bent down to drink some water from it. The cold breeze stung his chin and Jay lamented the beard that once grew long and flowing from his face. The cold of late November was not kind to the rest of his extremities, either. Jay had no idea where he was, or where he planned to go. Everything around him had an alien taste to it. The buildings were odd and pointy. The random and minute nature of the architecture of Nazareth had been replaced with dull uniformity. All the building looked the same which made navigating confusing and difficult. The people dressed in strange garments made from a variety of unfamiliar fabrics and colours. Jay had never seen anything like it. There wasn't a pair of sandals in sight. Instead, the people wore heavy chunks of rubber on their feet which were connected to unnecessarily tight trousers. Nobody looked comfortable and everyone seemed to conform to this standard of dress.

The loud carriages passed by ferociously and Jay wondered how they moved so quickly without being pulled by anything. As he walked aimlessly, taking in his bizarre new surroundings, he began to attract the attention of many passers-by. Having forgotten that he was naked despite the cold, Jay felt the eyes of many people on him. Many were laughing and several people shouted profanities, some that were familiar, and other words that he had never heard before.

It wasn't much longer before a loud carriage screeched to a halt on the road next to Jay. It was different from the others because it had flashing blue lights, and Jay marvelled at the impressive illusion. A man and a woman stepped out from within the carriage wearing the brightest colours Jay had ever seen. Noticing the richness of their fabrics, Jay guessed that they were part of the local aristocracy.

"Jesus Christ... Are you feeling okay, pal?" The man spoke, drawing out the ends of his words. His way of speaking was hard to understand but not impossible.

"Actually, most people just call me Jay, it is glorious to meet you on this fine day." Jay stretched out his hand to greet the man dressed in bright colours. The man followed suit, but just before they embraced, the neon-clothed elite grabbed the wrist of Jay's outstretched arm and twisted it around and into the lower back of Jay, causing him to wince in pain.

"I don't care what you're called fella, you can't be out here exposing yourself." Using his arm as a point of leverage, the man directed Jay to the back door of the car and guided him into a seated position. He placed sore metal bracelets tightly around Jay's wrists so that he didn't have use of his arms. The female officer had already begun talking into a small box in the front which squawked back at her with a muffled voice. Jay sat on the inside of the carriage, seemingly pleased to be having the experience. He was still very naked, a detail that he was either unaware of, or completely un-bothered by. He hung loosely on the warm leather. The neon female who controlled the carriage kept her eyes straight forward, doing her best not to steal a glance at the surprisingly handsome naked man in the back seat. Jay rubbed his legs with his restricted hands to warm himself. The woman looked at him through the small reflective mirror that hung from the roof.

"What's that on your hands, sir?" She took one hand off of the small wheel in front of her and drew a circle with her finger on the back of her other palm.

"Oh…" Jay looked down and saw a raw red circle in the centre of each of his palms. The circle appeared on either side of his palm, and had the new pinkness of scarred skin. The wrinkled look on his face gave away his uncertainty, and the woman impatiently averted her gaze again. It wasn't too long before the carriage came to a stop. They had arrived to wherever it was they were going. The man opened up the door and Jay wiggled his way out. Leaving the car, he suddenly became aware of his nakedness as the cold air attacked his vulnerability.

The man grabbed Jay firmly by the arm just above his elbow and guided him behind the woman who led them into the building. The entrance was wide and busy as many people bustled in and out like working bees. Many of them wore the same clothing as the two people that had apprehended Jay. They entered through the double doors with purpose. The man still held Jay's arm firmly. The entrance opened up into a large open space filled with the hustle of a busy day. The back wall was fronted by a line of counters, behind which stood more people in uniforms. The rest of the room consisted of more uniformed individuals sat at smaller desks throughout the space. There was a seating area to the left where both angry and scared-looking people hawked the uniformed elites. The large desk in front of the double doors had the words 'Precinct 84' sprawled across it in heavy black lettering. The woman chatted briefly to the uniform who sat behind the desk before the man guided Jay down a hallway off to the left and into a small room. The room was situated at the far end of the building. It contained one silver table, 2 chairs, and a mirror. The two neon-clad officers left Jay on his own in the room.

By now Jay had had quite some time to figure out what had happened to him, yet it was still very unclear. Remembering anything prior to waking up in the park naked was proving difficult. He knew for certain that he was no longer in Nazareth, and wondered whether he had been brought to Rome. It was certainly more advanced, and much stranger than his home. The last thing he could remember was his stag-do, which admittedly was also blurry. After he had rejoined the lads, they continued to drink quite heavily, and the next thing Jay knew, he was waking up naked in a strange place with strange marks on his hands. The most surprising part of it all was that he wasn't hungover in the slightest.

Before long the man who had initially captured Jay came back into the room. He held a small slab of wood in his hand, on top of which lied some paper. He sat down at the table opposite Jay and studied him, before throwing a dressing gown down in front of Jay.

"I have some questions to ask you. Put that on, please." He nodded to the gown on the table. They had released Jay's hands from the shackles once he had been put in the room, so Jay stood and put the gown on. The fabric was rough and itchy, but he welcomed the warmth.

"Alright then, let's get started," the man left out a long, exasperated breath as he scanned the paper in front of him. "Name?"

"Eh, Jason, but everyone calls me Jay, or Zeus, sometimes both. But Jay is fine just hasten with the Jason." Jay fidgeted with his hands as he spoke.

"Jay Zeus?"

"Zeus is my middle name. My mother was a bit mad. She was obsessed with Gods so she's the one to blame."

"Right. And do you have a surname? A last name?"

"Uh, where I live that's not usually done. It's usually Jay-Zeus of Nazareth because that's where I'm from." The officer put down his pen and glared at Jay.

"That's enough of the funny business, pal. I've had enough nut jobs come in here and try and tell me that they're the second coming of Jesus. Have you taken any drugs? Why are you naked? Why do you keep speaking like that?" His patience was wearing thin and the venom in his voice was obvious.

"I do apologies, sir, I'm not trying to waste your time. The last thing I remember was being with the lads drinking wine. Next thing I know, I'm waking up naked on the grass in that park. I have no idea what happened, sir, my memory's gone dark." Jay had a sincerity about the way he spoke. The officer put down the clipboard.

"OK sir, we're going to detain you overnight so that whatever you took has enough time to wear off. We'll then drive you to a shelter nearby in the morning. You'll be able to find yourself some clothes and food there. Hang on here for a few more minutes until I find a cell for you to stay in." The officer's brow furrowed as he took a final glance at Jay before leaving the room. Jay stared curiously at the empty seat across from him, still trying to put his memories together.

A different officer, this time a short, blonde-haired woman, brought Jay from the small room back into the main lobby. She escorted him to one of the small desks and sat him down. She guided Jay through pressing his thumb onto some dark blue ink, and then onto a specific sheet of paper. She did this for both hands. She then put the inked document, along with the details from his interview into a brown envelope and labelled it 'J.Z', before placing it on the tray at the corner of her desk. Jay was then taken to the back of the room, passed the countertops and into another hallway. Here the rooms had no doors, but instead the front wall of each was lined with thick steel bars; they were holding cells. Finally, there was something about this place that was perfectly familiar, and Jay was almost happy to see the cramped cells. They stopped about halfway down the long corridor in front of an empty cell. Jay was released from his hand shackles before being locked into the small room. He sat down on the edge of the narrow bench against the left-hand wall and closed his eyes. There was not much more he could do to figure out how he had gotten there. The next day would hopefully bring more answers. He moved onto his side and could feel the coldness of the concrete bench seeping through his thin robe. Nevertheless, the exhaustion soon took effect, and Jay dreamt of home and of the woman he was due to marry.

The following morning Jay waited patiently in his cell. The night's sleep hadn't done any favours for his memory. Shortly after 9AM the female officer who had helped to bring him in from the street arrived at the cell to leave him go.

"Inmate J.Z.?" She read the front of the brown envelope. "I'm bringing you down to the shelter this morning to get you some help." She escorted Jay to the noisy carriage they had arrived in and brought him the short distance through the giant buildings to the shelter situated two blocks away. The car sped away as Jay stepped onto the curb. Now with the fog of sleep shaken off, Jay was able to take in the full might of the city. The streets were saturated with people, each seemingly in a rush to be somewhere else. Not even the great Temple was ever this busy. The buildings were so big that Jay had to crane his neck to take in their full figure. Gazing up at the impossibly tall structures made him feel light-headed and wobbly. All around Jay there were scents, and voices and noises, all of which were unusual and strange. Merchants sold various wares and foods at apparently good prices. The city was truly alive and the energy filled Jay with an inexplicable sense of hope and excitement. He was amazed. He'd never been to a city so breathtaking. He imagined that the Kingdom of God itself wouldn't be so unbelievably grand.

"The shelter is situated on the corner of 42nd and Broadway", the officer had explained. Jay now found himself gazing up at a post of green signs, which marked that location. The doorway of the nearest building was jammed by a long queue, which snaked its way down the hallway to where there was another doorway into a large open room. The room was filled with cheap cots and it reminded Jay of the leper colony on the outskirts of Jerusalem.

Jay peered through the doorway and noticed that there was another, smaller queue leading to a small table to the right. Behind the table were racks and racks of clothing and shoes and coats and everything in between. Jay sidestepped the longer queue and joined this one instead. When he reached the top, the woman at the desk didn't say a word, but just handed Jay a bundle of clothes and pointed behind her to small area which had a screen to get changed behind. He pulled on some trousers made from denim that were too big and baggy which he secured to his thin waist with a belt. The woman had also given him a large t-shirt and hooded sweatshirt, both of which were too big for his skinny frame. Finally, he pulled on a heavy overcoat that had a fur-lined hood. Jay suddenly felt a lot more comfortable, now being fully dressed for the first time in over 24 hours. He reappeared from behind the screen and made his way back to the table.

"How do I look?" he asked the woman with a smile.

She glanced up, "Like a proper New Yorker".

"New Yorker, what is this?" Jay was visibly confused.

"New Yorker? You're in New York, honey. Don't ya know that?" She hadn't looked up from whatever she was writing.

"New York… a strange name for a beautiful city. This city seems like the place dreams are made of, is there nothing you cannot do here?"

"You're not wrong, honey, that's the perfect way to describe it. Anyone can be anything they want here." She looked up at Jay once more and considered him for a moment. "Hold on a second, hun." She turned around and rummaged through a nearby box before pulling out a navy hat. She turned back to Jay and handed it to him, "This'll make you look right at home."

Jay examined the item. It was completely navy with a straight bill at the front. The only feature of note was some white embroidery on the front with the letters 'NY' stitched on top of one another. He squeezed it onto his head and could feel the pressure of the tight hat on his temples.

"The Yankees, baby. New York's favourite team." The lady winked at Jay before moving to help the next person in line.

Jay stood, deep in thought for a moment before the sounds all around brought him straight back into reality. He made his way for the exit again and paused outside, to take in the busy city once more. Then, pulling his Yankee hat tighter onto his head, Jay began to walk forward with the crowd, into the concrete jungle to see what the city had to offer.

How are things?
All good and yourself?
Ah sure driving it on, can't complain
Fair play.

Nug-Life Sentence

Norman Gordonson won the same award at his company's end of year party every holiday season. It had become something of a tradition. A reliable constant in a world that was spun up in relentless turmoil. Norman, or 'Normy' as his mother called him, accepted his award each year in the same dull and uninteresting suit, which had not been updated in the 15 years that he had worked at Indisputable Insurance Ltd. *"Most Job Appropriate Name"*, was the award Norman accepted each December with a consistent level of awkwardness and unease. He disliked the award, but was not so unaware that he didn't know why he had earned it. See, Norman was an Insurance Actuary, which isn't the most exciting of jobs, and Norman wasn't the most exciting of people. Quite the opposite really. Norman Harold Gordonson was 44 years old. He had never left the country, and rarely left the county. He lived with his mother (Although he'd argue that she lived with him) in the same house he grew up in. He had never taken a wife, having found out quite early on in life that he was, "aggressively infertile", according to the evaluation of several doctors. His wardrobe consisted of the same exact work outfit times five, and the same exact casual outfit times 3, in case there was a long weekend. Norman only ate stews and shepherd's pies, and he only ever drank one specific brand of bottled water, as they didn't add as much fluoride as other brands. He rarely took holidays from work, and would rather be paid the extra money directly into his savings account instead of taking the days off. The only source of unpredictability in his life was his pet tortoise, Mervyn, who didn't stick to a schedule as acutely as Norman would like him to. This was the one characteristic of Mervyn that Norman wasn't entirely fond of, but he knew nobody was perfect, and Mervyn was damn near close.

It will come as no surprise then that Norman Gordonson thoroughly enjoyed his job. It was a highly predictable, highly logic-based form of work. Every small decision required detailed paperwork, and Norman couldn't think of a better way to pass an afternoon than filing the various forms correctly. He specialized in car insurance primarily, but Norman was so anal about his work that he was often called into other departments to consult. He was an insurance company's wet dream, as his claims-approval rating was outstandingly low due to his 'by-the-book' nature. Norman's life was, to anyone other than Norman, intolerably boring, but that's how he liked it. He was as bland as they come. Therefore, the last thing Norman Gordonson ever expected, or wished upon himself, was to be cast into the public eye. However, on Tuesday, April 23rd, 2019 Norman was handed an insurance claim that would become the focus of the media on a global scale.

On the surface of it all, the claim seemed like a run of the mill, standard procedure. There had been a small collision on the intersection of quite a busy roundabout. No parties were injured, and so it was a simple claim to repair damages. The tail end of one car was written off, as was the front end of the car that had collided with it. Norman had expected the owner of the front car to be claiming off the insurance of the car which had hit from behind, as was the status quo. However, as Norman read through the documentation he began to realize there was something askew about this case. The owner of the rear car was claiming from the front car's insurance which was unusual but not without precedent. But that was far from the strangest part. The owner of the front car had submitted a lawsuit claim against a very profitable fast-food chain for a life time's supply of; Chicken Nuggets.

Norman cleaned his spectacles on his shirt and took a moment to steady himself. What on Earth had that fast-food chain to do with a fender-bender? It made no sense. The irregularity of the entire situation made Norman feel quite uneasy, as he realised he'd have to evoke more intensive investigative methods to get to the bottom of this. Amongst the paperwork for this case was the report from the Garda who arrived upon the scene, Garda Michelle Fitzpatrick. She wrote:

April 22nd 2019

*A collision occurred at approximately 12:10
PM on entrance to the Kinsale Road Roundabout from the Turners Cross side, resulting in
one 2009 Ford Focus and one 131 Toyota
Avensis being written off as not roadworthy.
The driver of the Ford Focus, Helen Gallagher,
wishes to claim off of the insurance of the drive
of the Avensis, Arthur McArthur. Ms. Gallagher
claims that the collision occurred due to
McArthur's "Sudden and unnecessary braking" which resulted in the Ford Focus colliding
into the back of the Avensis. McArthur wishes
to claim off of, or sue, McDonald's for negligence. The insurance information was taken
from both parties and the decision as to how to
proceed is to be left to the relevant insurance
companies.*

Norman was baffled. Negligence? What on Earth did
McDonald's do in this circumstance to cause a car
crash. It made literally no sense. The contact information for both parties, McArthur and Gallagher were also
in the file. Norman picked up the receiver on the edge
of his desk and dialled the first number. After 3 rings
that phone call engaged.

"How'sa goin'?"

"Hi, is this Arthur McArthur?

"Yeah this is himself. What's the story?"

Mr. McArthur, My name is Norman Gordonson. I'm
an actuary at Indisputable Insurance and I was assigned
to your case. I must admit I'm quite confused by some

of the details of the situation. Is it true that you're intending to sue McDonald's for causing the accident?"

"Ah lethal, lethal. I'll tell ya know like, the crash wouldn't have happened if it weren't for McDonald's like, so surely they have to cough up? As in, I can't afford for my own premium to go up anymore and it wasn't my fault, you know what I mean'?"

"Sorry Mr. McArthur, how has McDonald's anything to do with this case? You weren't anywh-"

"Stall on now a second and I'll explain. I was already chatting to a lawyer about it, and she reckons there's a good chance we'll get a pay-out. So, I'd just been into that new drive through over by Musgrave park or Independence park? Whatever it's called anyway you know the one. I got myself a 20 box of nuggets and some barbeque sauce, sweet chili and all that, they give you four or five dips like it's savage. That was grand anyway. I zipped out of there happy-days like and was munching away and the aul' barbecue sauce fucking fell off of the passenger seat. Well, it more of less flew off really as I was turning there to come onto the roundabout and it scared the living daylights out of me because I thought it was a bat or something in the car, so I braked naturally out of fear as you would. Yer wan behind me must have been up my hole anyway because she came flying into the back of me and sure didn't the nuggets go all over the gaff then. Look I'm not blaming her either it's McDonald's fault anyway. That's the craic now.

"And in what way do you think McDonald's are liable?" Norman couldn't hide how shocked he was at what he was hearing.

"Well like, they shouldn't be serving food to people who are driving really. As in, it's fairly irresponsible letting people be distracted by food whilst driving. If I'd never been able to get the nuggets in the first place the barbecue sauce wouldn't have startled me and I woulda never used the brakes, get me? So I think it's only fair that they sort out the two cars and give us a life supply of nuggets for my troubles."

There was an inexplicably long pause as Norman gathered his thoughts. There was a certain logic to what Mr. McArthur was saying, which frightened the middle-aged actuary more than anything else. Seeing as there was a chance that the crash was caused by their chicken nuggets, Norman would have no choice but to file a lawsuit on behalf of his client against the monster fast-food company, a suit that would undoubtedly be snapped up by the media due to the high profile of the company, and the outright absurdity of the story.

"That's all we need from you at this time, Mr McArthur. We'll be in contact with you as the case proceeds." Norman hung up the phone and dabbed away the sweat that was now pooling on his large forehead. He reached for the decanter of water and spilt water on his trousers as he poured himself a glass. His hands were shaking violently as he tried to calm himself with the drink. Taking extraordinary measures made Gordonson extremely uncomfortable, and this was certainly the most extraordinary of circumstances.

As it turned out, there was precedent for situations like this; an awful lot of precedent. All over the world, there were claims, and lawsuits filed against various fast food chains due to product related accidents. It was unbelievable. Nevertheless, as soon as the local press got wind of the pending lawsuit, the entire country was talking about it. The hashtag '#NugLife' was trending in Ireland for months as the trial proceeded. Norman couldn't leave his own house without being bombarded by questions from the press eagerly waiting outside. Everyone wanted to know why he'd decided to pursue the case rather than pay out the €850 that was the resulting damage of the fender bender. Norman had only responded once with a quote from one of his favourite wizards of all time, Albus Dumbledore. "Dark times lie ahead of us and there will be a time when we must choose between what is right and what is easy."

The quote went viral and Norman was nicknamed by the press as the Half-Nug Prince from then on. The trial was dragged out for months by incredibly dull and pedantic lawyering. Neither side seemed to have a firm grip on winning the complex court battle. There was an offer to settle which would have resulted in both cars being replaced by the fast food chain, as well as a year's supply of chicken nuggets for both parties involved in the small accident. However, Mr. McArthur's lawyers refused the offer, claiming that it was a matter of justice for the everyday man that Arthur McArthur receive his full lifetime supply.

Norman 'The Half Nug Prince' was woken by the phone ringing on a warm September's morning, almost 5 months into the trial. He answered the phone, his eyes still crisp with sleep.

"Good morning Mr. Gordonson", the voice was familiar but hard to place.

"This is John Jensen of Johnson & Jensen Attorneys. I'm calling on behalf of our mutual client, Arthur McArthur. The trial didn't end so well. It got dirty, some undisclosed information was uncovered. McArthur is on his way to prison.

"Jesus Christ, what on Earth happened?"

"I can't say much right now but I'm sure it'll come up in the press. The authorities will probably bring you in for questioning soon. That's all I can say for now." The line went dead. It wouldn't be long before Norman found out exactly what had happened.

Nearly every newspaper had the story slapped onto the front page, eagerly displaying pictures of the man who Norman had known to be Arthur McArthur. His real name was John C. Whiteman, but most people knew him by his nickname; The Colonel. His great, great, great grandfather has begun his own fast food company back in the day, and John Whiteman was the heir to it all. The whole court case was the latest attempt to bring down the powerhouse of the fast food industry, but it fell short when the private investigators hired to dig into Arthur McArthur uncovered the truth. The Colonel had been embedded in Cork for well over 6 years, planning and carrying out what ended up as quite a lazy attempt at attacking the burger slinging juggernaut. Ironically enough, Arthur McArthur AKA John C. Whiteman AKA The Colonel earned himself a stay at prison that lasted for as many years as there are chicken nuggets in the largest portion you can order at

McDonald's; 20. The New York Times captured the story perfectly with the headline, "Nug Life Sentence For the Kentucky Kid".

As for Norman Gordonson, it didn't end quite as badly. Due to his popularity in the media as 'The Half-Nug Prince', Norman was offered a book deal which would be the tell-all for the very bizarre lawsuit which he found himself caught up in, and the role that Norman played in it all. It was ear-marked to be the bestseller of the year. However, in true Norman Gordonson style, the book showed absolutely no character whatsoever, and turned out to be very boring indeed.

Once you notice a person's eyebrows it's almost impossible to listen to what they're saying.

Trust me.

Pedro

Plenty of reasons not to go there. Plenty of reasons to just stay here and leave it off. Will anyone notice that you skipped out? Probably not. Brendo, or one of the others might text but you can just say you fell asleep early or something. It'll be grand. Don't worry about it at all. Nobody actually cares if you're there or not. Just sink back into the bed there now and take it handy. It's just gone 9 which means it's almost 10 which is a perfectly acceptable time to go to bed at your age. You're 27 like, you're not as young as you have been. You're grand, stay in bed there now for yourself.

The mother would have to head taken clean off me if she knew I stopped taking my pills. I'm used to the anxious thoughts, so this was a perfectly regular stream of consciousness for me on a Friday night. What was not regular was that the words were being delivered by my pet Golden Retriever, Pedro, in a snooty London accent. That part was very new. He was quite literally looking down his long nose at me. Pedro had jumped up on the bed next to me and started lecturing me on why I should stay in. The absurdity of the situation left me frozen in place. You'd expect yourself to scream at the sound of a talking Golden Retriever, but no. I just sat there and took it. There was nobody else in the house and nobody was gonna believe me when I told them this had happened. I probably wouldn't tell anyone anyway. I wasn't so far gone that I wasn't aware that I was clearly hallucinating. Weening myself off the meds clearly had some sort of adverse effect on my brain because now I was straight up seeing things. Pedro licked my face before he left my room and that was that.

Later that night I woke up pissing the bed. There was a brief moment of relief before the smell of concentrated urine corrupted my airways and I realised I was still lying down. I got up and ran to the bathroom but the tank was more or less empty by the time I got there. As I stripped off my pissy pyjamas I heard Pedro's claws clacking on the timber floorboards as he passed by the bathroom. I could also hear him chuckling away to himself at my expense. My own dog was laughing at me. I jumped into the shower, no longer sleepy, and pressed the button for water. The shower head gushed needlessly cold water at me without warning. My pulse went through the roof and the wind was knocked completely out of me.

I woke up in a cold sweat, gasping for air. The whole thing had been a dream, and I sighed with relief. My sheets were drenched with sweat, which was cold and wet. I turned on my bedside lamp to inspect where, if anywhere, there was a dry patch for me to sleep on. Turning on the lamp, I got another fright as Pedro appeared from out of the darkness in the corner of my room, pissing on a pair of my shoes. He paused briefly, having been caught and there was a silent tension between us. We both maintained eye-contact for well over 40 seconds. He called me a pussy before continuing to piss on my Nikes, and I turned the lamp back off.

Morning light struck my body through the thin curtains and began the wakefulness system churning within my body. I woke 6 minutes before my alarm, in the damp, swamp that was my bed. Waking in this environment was a regular occurrence, and it made no odds to me. I stripped off my heavy t-shirt, the ring of sweat still visible around the neck, finished in a triangle in the centre of my chest. I opened the window to air out my bedroom as the mixed scent of sweat and dog piss was quite overbearing. There was a bottle of water by the window that I drank from to cure the dryness of my mouth. I noticed I had set my alarm 2 hours later than usual and so, although I had woken before the alarm I was still extremely late for work. I screamed to the clouds and cursed the Gods as the post-woman handed me that morning's delivery. She seemed nervous and I couldn't remember getting outside. My dressing-gown was soaked as the rain pelted down in a patronising reply to my scolding.

There were no letters for me but several Late Notice letters for my parents. Mother wasn't home but Father was, so I opened the freezer and threw the letters into him. His cold, dead eyes glazed through me, and he didn't utter a word of thanks. I slammed the freezer shut and gave a guttural roar before throwing a left hook into the kitchen wall. The solid concrete put a stop to my anger as I reeled in pain. Blood oozed from my middle knuckle and I wrapped a sock I found on the radiator around my fist to stop the bleeding. At that very moment Pedro trotted by and called me a prick. He can be a gas cunt.

The smell of burning human flesh had become something of a treat to my nostrils. I hadn't ever imagined that burning 4 corpses would take more than one sitting. The fifth fire was the last of it, though. Pedro was nearby, chewing on the bone of one of my brother's, or maybe it was belonged to my mother. It was impossible to tell at this stage. The phone had been ringing mad a lot lately, so Pedro told me to disconnect it. He's a smart dog in fairness to him. That night Pedro woke up to me pissing on him. Nobody gets away with destroying my shoes without pay-back. He appreciated the fight in me and cleaned himself quietly.

The police showed up the next day. They said that some of my relatives had been in touch, concerned that they hadn't heard from anyone in over a week. I told them I thought my parents had gone on holidays and that my older sister and younger brother were likely to be anywhere, and that they did their own thing. I also told them I'd lost my glasses but in reality I knew exactly where they were. They seemed to believe I was telling the truth. Both officers refused my invitation to join me for tea in the back garden. One of them wished me luck finding my glasses as they left and I laughed my thanks back in his direction. I could hear Pedro enjoying his viewing of The Chase inside as I waved away the police officers.

As dusk rolled around that same day, I could hear the police sirens howling from about 4 miles away. It sounded like at least 3 cars judging by the overlapping wails of authority. I unlocked the front door and began to undress as I walked back in towards the kitchen. Dressed now only in underwear, I took as many heads from the chest-freezer as I could manage, and placed them on the kitchen table. There were 7 on the counter and it looked like there was about 15 more still in the freezer. I couldn't even remember killing some of them, which was concerning, but it didn't matter too much. I hadn't sleep-walked since I was a kid. I turned one of the kitchen chairs toward the open front door and sat down. I pointed a finger-gun in its direction. Pedro shook his head at me and called me a coward. The fury of the sirens erupted into the driveway and I could hear the shouting of manly men and women bustling towards the house. They came in and shouted at me repeatedly to get on the ground. They handled me quite roughly and called me names and one of the men hit me with the butt of his lovely hand-gun. I went quietly and politely with them, yet they still look disgusted, which I thought was quite rude.

You'd be surprised how quickly your sadness will dissipate by exercising daily and drinking your water.

A truly magical combination.

Fallout

I always loved how falling snow wasn't sure of itself. It blew here and there and up and around, unable to decide where it should be. It was the snow that fell between the blizzard and the sleet. It was snow that didn't really know what it was to become just yet. It was my favourite snow and I could sit for hours, watching it through the window, as it fell in its indecisive way, covering the garden in its pureness. The slow that fell now wasn't like that. It fell heavily, with dead certainty. It was grey and wet and it made the ground turn into a thick black sludge that was impossible to move. It turns the grass into muck instead of into a crisp white blanket. This was our snow now.

I no longer sat at the window and watched the snow, the snow that never seemed to stop. It fell constantly, covering the ground in horrible mud. It dulled the light of the sun, which nobody had really seen in the open in what felt like an eternity. The greyness fell and fell, a permanent reminder of the past, a dull and consistent memory. The days trickled by as such like the drip of a faulty faucet. Maintaining a calendar was no longer relevant, as each day was the same as last and as the one to follow. The greyness and the cold and the monotony should have driven us to death, but we all lived with that hope. A hope that one day the grey, burning snow would stop. A hope that stepping foot outside didn't mean certain death. A hope that we might see pure snow again, dancing in the breeze with a lightness that life seemed to have forgotten.

I spent my days reading. Once the morning chores were done, once we had fed everyone, and sent the children to run their errands and then into the education centre, I spent my days reading, and thinking and sometimes writing. In between reading shifts I helped prepare the meals and asked around to see if anyone needed anything done. I helped to draw metallic tasting water from the deep well and snuck extra mouthfuls when the leader turned his back. When the odd jobs were done I'd go back to my room and get lost once more in what books remained. I used the words of Plato and Joyce and Nietzsche and Descartes and Dickens to escape from the dull drone of the new world. I found solace in their words and wisdom in their prose and I often wondered if there were one of them amongst those of us left here to survive it all. I wondered if someone like them had perished with the billions of others who hadn't made it. It made me sad to think of these things but it also made me cherish their works even more feverishly and I spent my time away from my books excited to return.

Often I'd spend my time drawing inspiration from my idols, trying to work back through the philosophers and the scholars and the scientists to see where and why we had taken a turn for the worse. I tried to use their theories to understand how we'd traded green pastures and life for acidic waters and death. How had we let our world come to this?

I considered the history books that had been salvaged, as few as there were. The Industrial Revolution in Britain to me seemed like a milestone that turned humanity into something toxic, but from studying the sophists and Kant I figured that this revolutionary time of ideas couldn't itself have been inherently right or wrong, and that it was what humanity did with its new technology that may have turned the world into chaos. Therefore, although the Industrial Revolution seemed obvious, it may not have been the hinging point. Industrial civilisation resulted in advancements in warfare, taking humanity from the bow and arrow to propulsion weaponry, and the cost of life from war after then was unprecedented. Nevertheless, humanity got through its warring phase seemingly unharmed, even with all the threats of nuclear destruction throughout the 20th Century between The USA and USSR. It seemed to my, admittedly flawed mind that whatever caused us to become what were now happened after we had figured out that annihilating one another was not the best course towards progress.

There were, of course, major cavities in my knowledge. History had up until now, never been of any interest to me. Perhaps this was because I rest assured knowing someone else was taking care of it. They were taking the time to carefully analyse and document every minute detail and making sense of what had come before us, like fitting together the pieces of a forever morphing puzzle. But now, when all we had left were some tattered textbooks and a handful of philosophy manuscripts, now it seems essential to record what had gone before so that whatever happened to us wouldn't repeat itself. We had been reduced to the brink of extinction. Perhaps there were more colonies out there, but with no means of communication, it was futile to fixate on this possibility. We only knew us, so for all intents and purposes, there was only us.

So if it wasn't the revolution of industry that caused it then it must be something that happened after that. There were world wars, cold wars, wars on drugs, wars on terror, wars on religion. There was no shortage of opportunity for the world to end in the 20th Century. Between the threat of nuclear war and the AIDS crisis of the 80s and the terrorism that became rampant in the beginning decades of the 21st Century, it is surprising to me that this isn't the source of our current existence. Although, it is possible, and indeed likely, that the person, or people that were involved in bringing about our predicament were born and lived through some of these events. They endured the brutality of Al Qaeda's and ISIS and maybe even the Vietnam War and the Iraq war and the Cold War between Russia and America. They were alive for the most interesting time in human history and one can only speculate on how living through that affects the way a person might think. They'd not have the moral certainty of Kant, or the wisdom of Socrates or the humility of Aquinas. They'd have no appreciation of the moral integrity of generations by-gone. How could they? How could you expect them to?

Still, the actions of these people would have reper-cussions that would affect the lives of millions for gen-erations, well after they went for the long sleep. Well after they repented for the sins, their actions would still wreak havoc. How do we reconcile that? How do we forgive these people for isolating us all and causing acidic snow to fall for more than 50 years? Maybe we don't. Maybe we don't forgive but we do learn. But maybe we will never truly learn from these errors if we don't achieve genuine forgiveness. Without forgiveness, we may never truly understand the reasons for their ac-tions and without that knowledge are we not doomed to someday repeat what they did to us?

It wasn't something that had happened in that trialling 20th Century. You'd have put your money there if you were a betting man. But no. The millennium passed without a hitch in its step, despite all the arbitrary fear about that 2000th year. The smoothness was short lived though. The beginning of the 21st Century brought with it a new wave of terrorist warfare. The events of 9/11 shook the entire Western world to the gut. The war on terror became the primary war. It became the front for American forces to exploit the Middle East for oil rich lands too, though. Still, although this new era of terror brought along many more complex issues, it itself didn't get us here. It did however birth a reinvigorated anti-immigrant mentality as a new wave of xenophobic values took hold on the populations of many countries.

When a man named Barack Obama got voted in as the first black President of America, however, it seemed like the tide was turning. Not that he was an immigrant, but his election suggested that the people of the most powerful country on Earth had moved past bigotry and the small mindedness of the previous century. There are accounts in one of the more modern textbooks we have, testimonials from social commentators that suggested the contrary. They said that because we were still noting the colour of a person's skin, making it novel and important, that the racist and bigoted attitudes of our predecessors were still present but had become latent and benign. They said that to achieve a true world without racism, people wouldn't see the colour of skin but only the merit of one's character. And so, although progress appeared to have been made, it was simply over-correction to mask the truth.

This hidden truth became clarified with the president that followed Obama. A man voted in based on the fact that he was outright about his bigotry and his ability to 'tell it like it is'. Donald Trump was the President of America for back-to-back terms. A feat so unbelievable, if you were to take the progressive nature of the internet as representative. Nevertheless, Trump was re-elected, and that is where things took a turn for the worst.

Now before you get to your assumptions, you'll either be offended or delighted to know that Trump is not the reason we find ourselves in a nuclear winter, almost 60 years after the fact. Trump didn't do this, but something he suggested half-heartedly without a second thought did inspire someone to save a country. This attempt at heroism is the entire reason humanity finds itself in the position it now occupies. Which makes our desperate fate so ironic; our demise came about from the purest idiotic intentions.

Presidents are sources of inspiration. That almost goes without saying. I think we've too often assumed that this inspiration can only be good. But when a president is negligent, that produces negligent inspiration. This inspiration is corrupted, so to speak. We no longer have presidents. Why would we? There are only a few thousands of us now, so decisions can be made fairly decidedly. So, I guess we can say that Donald Trump was the source of our demise but not the cause of it. I don't think the history books of the past would have made that distinction, though. History is generally written by the victor, But I am neither victor nor loser. I was born after it all happened, and so I can only perceive second hand accounts. This history will be written by the indifferent, by the ones who knew no reprise but only wish to know truth.

So President Trump inspired the events that caused us to fall into nuclear fallout. That much is clear from the textbooks we still have in our library. He inspired another world leader, the dictator in North Korea, to take radical measures to battle the quickly progressing climate issue. What Trump said had no grounds in science whatsoever, which based off the information I've been able to glean on Donald Trump, wasn't an uncommon thing for him to do. He just said this thing and got ridiculed by the internet and the scientific community. And yet, his counterpart on the other side of the world, took this information and acted on it in an attempt to save his kingdom from an atmosphere that would bring the country to ruin.

From the summer of 2022, North Korea, as well as many other countries, began to be bombarded by hurricane, after hurricane, in an era known as 'The Greater Depression'. By the end of 2023, North Korea had experienced 12 hurricanes within 18 months. A thirteenth would have brought the state's economy to its knees, which, as we know from the archives, was an economy that was already as frail as a house of cards. Left with no other options, due to an almost non-existent department of climate scientists, Kim Jong-un recalled the confident words of his friend, Donald Trump. On the 14th of January 2024, Jung-Un made the call. He took the codes that were locked away in his presidential palace and keyed them into the launch module that had been summoned from the Air Base in Pyongyang. On that day, Kim turned two keys simultaneously by himself, and launched five nuclear missiles directly into the eye of the hurricane that was looming only kilometres off the western shoreline of North Korea.

Sometimes poems don't rhyme
And none of these poems are poems
So the joke's on you, dork.

The Scent of Sunshine

She'd fallen asleep in the grass again. The sun always wore her out entirely. Her naps in the sun were some of the better ones. She'd awake in a drowsy confusion, the birds enchanting the air, the sun still lapping at her thick hair. A fresh groan and a stretching out of the front limbs would scatter the near-by robins, before she'd sit back down, upright and glancing around to investigate the goings-on. Long ears stood at attention and analysing the chaos of noises.

Here she comes. Pale and tiny and giggling. "Tawha!" she'd scream in excitement. Close enough. Tara stood and the tail wagged her affection, and she bounded for the little girl and prodded her hands with a wet nose. A request for rubs was approved without hesitation. Tara licked the little girl's face with a warm, tongue that was everywhere and the girl shook out a warble of laughter and Tara's tail wagged even faster in the warmth of a summer's day.

Days when the little blonde girl came were always sunny and full of rubs and playing. Often Tara waited at the front door for her to come. Sometimes she didn't come. On those days, Tara roamed the back garden and chased birds and barked at passing cars that she could hear from the road, and she drank cool water in the sunshine. Tara could pick up the smell of her from down the road when she was on her way, and she ran and jumped at the sliding porch door to be let in, and she barked and ran and wagged in excitement.

The days when the little blonde girl came were pure bliss. When they'd both been worn out from playing, the little girl would sneak Tara inside, and they'd sleep together on the carpeted floor of the back room. The girl would cuddle into Tara's stomach and Tara would feel her heartbeat and the slowing of her breath. And the scent of the girl would be strong in her nostrils, and then scent now only reminded Tara of playing outside on sunny days, and she wondered if that was also how sunshine smelled.

When the darkness began to come more quickly in the day, and Tara could see the shapes of her barks in the air, the girl came less often. When she did come, it was either too dark, or cold, or wet to be outside, so they'd sit together inside and watch TV. Not as much fun as play outside, but Tara found herself to be quite happy with the little girl next to her, and the little girl's hand playing with her ears. She'd often get the best naps she ever had on these days, and the girl would stay right there as she dreamed.

The pair grew bigger together. Tara no longer stumbled over her legs. Soon, the little girl was no longer little. She began to shout 'Tara' instead of 'Tawha'. She was too big to jump on Tara now, and Tara was too old to want it. The periods of affectionate rubbing became shorter and more formal. They started going on walks, out on the boreens that surrounded the house. They still spent time but that time was spent less often and in different ways. They'd grown up together.

The sunny days turned into darker days and turned into sunnier days again. The little girl who used to fall asleep on Tara's back in the cool afternoons of summer no longer existed. She had to bend down now to reach Tara. She no longer hugged Tara, or spent hours running and talking to her in senseless excitement. The girl still smelled of sunshine, though. And sometimes when she was there, and she looked at Tara directly, Tara could see the eyes of the little girl looking back at her. And Tara would nudge her face again with her wet nose and the woman would allow a giggle. The same sound that used to make Tara yelp with happiness, the same laughter that the little girl used to make.

When the darkness began to draw in faster again, and the air would be biting and jagged, Tara felt a stiffness. Running became a painful engagement. On bad days, standing was even difficult. The little girl didn't call as often. Tara would wait for the smell of her all day, but it rarely came. Her fleeting visits became less frequent and when she was there, she rarely had the time for Tara, who prodded her hands at the kitchen table and was only given a short greeting in return. The little girl was different now too. She covered her head with hats and her eyes were deep in her head. She was skinny and always tired and never there. They'd sit on the couch together in the afternoons in their stiffness and sleep in an unspoken melancholy. The little girl would look down at Tara with sad eyes and massage her ears like

129

she always would, and Tara would groan quietly in contentment.

Not long after then, in the days between the darkness and the sun, there were many people in the house. Tara paced the garden and looked in the glass and barked at all the people in their dark shades and odd shapes. She raised her nose to understand through smell. And there were many smells, all tangled together in a cacophony of sweat and salt and wetness. But Tara couldn't smell the little girl. She couldn't smell the sunshine dwelling within, so she lay in the grass and dozed off in confused disinterest.

The sunny days came, and the darkness, and the in-between days, and the little girl never returned. Tara looked for her with her nose every day but her smell was nowhere. Tara grew older and sadder and stiffer. She no longer had the energy nor desire to play. She just sat in the grass on sunny days and remembered the little girl. And she remembered how she used to smell like sunshine felt, but the sun hadn't felt the same in a long time.

> *If you face your demons in the daytime*
> *Then you won't fear them in the night*
> *Unless*
> *Your demons ARE the night-time*
> *Then you're screwed.*

Home Visit

Leant there against the wall wearing the smugness of a taunting cat driving trapped dogs to madness, Bonnie took in the burnt yellow ocean expanding in front of him. The smirk stretching his lips halted briefly to allows a drag of smoke between his graveyard of teeth. A wicked charm he had, the type of face that'd have your mother infatuated. The constant stubble that suggested a degree of nonchalance was carefully orchestrated. His eyes sparkled with the comfort of a tropical ocean.

He kept one hand in the pocket of his long Autumn jacket, casual, like. The other, still cradling a rollie, slicked back his long fringe from his forehead to meet the freshly undercut buzzed-skin on the side of his head. Back to the wall, legs crossed one over the other and breathing in the freshness of the evening, Bonnie lived with the confidence of a fella who might get ahead of himself. The fields spread in front of him, nourished by the morning sun. The sweet scent of new slurry was an over-powering stinger. Despite himself, despite trying to escape his rural roots, Bonnie-lad relished the smell of the pig manure, the smell of a grand welcome home.

It had been a cool minute since he'd been back to the muck of it all. Chasing notions up in the big town was how his father had put it. The man had a heavy-handed understanding driven into him by a lifetime of Catholic shame. He held himself to no purpose higher than an honest day's work. He smiled now at Bonnie and palmed the side of the boy's face with a working man's grasp. The swelling of years of hard labour left him with hands unable to form proper fists and Bonnie could feel the rough welts graze his cheek. Bonnie re-coiled briefly and slicked his hair again, and the father chuckled as he walked on and into the back garden. His gait like that of an aging bull-terrier.

Yid wanna go inside and tell your mudder yer here and get that gowl of a jacket off ya, there's work needs doin'.

The father was tailed by a jet black Labrador called Saint. Tail wagging following the alpha about with a tongue struggling to escape his mouth. Bonnie exhaled on the flick of the cigarette from his fingertips and pulled himself off the wall. Two days was all he was home for. His patience was already stretching taught.

Bonnie glided into the kitchen with his face already wincing in anticipation. She couldn't control herself, God love her. Always got up in a heap and loved a good surprise and all.

Are ye well? Bonnie announced himself to the kitchen. There was a distant 'Jaysus' and the shuffling of heavy-set feet and a squeal of breathless delight. She was over showering Bonnie with wet kisses and hugs, and he grimaced but couldn't help but smile at the aul one's joy. She was gas out. Within minutes, she'd the tea on the table with a few scones and was asking for all the news on college in the big city and if there were any girleens on the scene and saying none of them'd be good enough for her handsome boy. Bonnie told her to relax that there was no girl to be worrying about just yet and the mother seemed oddly pleased about that.

The stove was in the corner pummelling heat into the tawny two-storey. A fine lump of local Wesht turf burning away in there, heating the house with centuries of tradition. You could smell the heat when you walked into the den, a metallic waft of man-made energy. Bonnie landed himself on the small wooden-framed armchair on the opposite side of the room to the stove.

Christ, Mam, it's absolutely roashtin' in here.

Sure wouldn't you be complaining too if it were too cold, Bon? Tisn't it lovely to be able to come home to the warmth of it? Wisht out that. The mudder bundled herself around to the stove and heaped another few dirty coal lumps into the stove. The father lurched through the sliding door, closing it behind him to the dismay of an agitated Saint who started barking a chorus of objections straight away.

Pipe down out there, you gowleen of a madra. Máire, is the kettle boiled, tis? A cuppa be lovely now before I take in the cattle.

The mudder jumped up at the sound of her hardworker. Sit down inside, Martin, I'll fix the tea, you must be shattered, boy.

The father came in and put himself into a chair opposite his son with his joints screaming. It was an old, battered couch that had been there since Bonnie could re-member.

Are you gonna get a haircut at all, boy, or are we gonna have the shart callin' you by a geril's name? He started laughing with the smoker's wheeze at his own joke. Bonnie, didn't dignify the question with a re-sponse. He stood and roared into the mother that he was going down the chipper if they wanted anything.

A chicken Maryland, Bon, with the curry on the side and a fish uh the day for your father. I'll fix you up af-ter.

Bonnie welcomed the break away from the cramped farmhouse and exhaled a relieving breath as he made his way up the drive-way. T'was still stretching out and the village was only a short jaunt, so he decided he'd walk it to lengthen his time away from the gaff. T'was only a weekend visit, two days only. A cloudy distilla-tion of a hometown visit served in a short glass.

The town hugged the coil of an old river off towards the Atlantic and onto the far side of that pond. The fog smouldered in on the regular. Fierce bravado off it but otherwise unintimidating. It burned off most morning by noon, laying low on the river in fear of the sunlight of the early summer. The town knew what it was when t'was needed of it, but it was otherwise confused. It was kebab shops and pulled-pork and donuts and dodgey tanning places. It was fowl-mouth youths and bitter old-wans. You'd be in a bad way if you found yourself on the wrong side of that river. But at the core of that small haven off the coast was music. That town survived off the hum and whine of a bosca ceoil. It thrived on the thumb-finger of a guitar out the back of Paddy Macs of a Thursday evening. The harmonica and flute jams on the square on the bend of River Fiachara outside Mary O's were legendary, bless us. That town was a confused bastard, but by God, it knew how to handle itself when there was a rhythm in the air.

Bonnie made his way from the farm along the cattle-track of a road into town. The road had a column of grass up the middle of it and that feature almost made Bonnie fond of the place. Not much of anything going on ever on these roads. The petrol station appeared on the far side of the river as Bonnie approached the foot-bridge that connected the bogland farms to the main centre of the town. The footbridge was often used as the battlegrounds for many a brawl between rival youths. Usually over some girl or because something was said of another fella's sister. Bonnie had been an athletic youth and was quiet enough so boys generally left him to it. But he still had memories of the rush of a chase across that footbridge and off into the darkness of the farmlands. Some gowl from up the Jameson Boreen felt Bonnie had a fine notion of himself that rubbed him the wrong way.

Bonnie smirked at the memory now as he came to passing the garage. He could smell the greasy batter and oil of the chipper already. Friday night would see it hectic out but Noreen's was one of those rare chip shops that was worth the wait. He passed the petrol station on his left and stayed with the road as it veered right up to Cromwell Street. He saluted the bronze statue of Gretel's Heffer as he skipped past it by the post office (As

135

was tradition). Bonnie felt the saliva build in his mouth as he made out the jagged sign for Noreen's on the corner. The queue didn't look too bad as it happened.

The heat from the deep fat fryers cradled your face as you welcomed yourself into the chipper, the bell rattling above the door to announce your entrance. The menu was as it always was, but Bonnie didn't even look up for it, he knew the order. Francis was on anyway, and she knew the order never changed. She winked at Bonnie as she caught the rhythm of his gaatch.

How ya, college boy? Been awhile hah? Same as always? She spoke to everyone with a sentimentality that gave you a weird pang of longing for home.

Same as always, Fran, thanks. Been busy with college stuff, only down for the weekend. Bonnie liked Francis, she was always full of chat.

Ah sure there's no keeping up with you, boy. Tell your mother I was asking for her. She turned away again to shake the baskets of piping hot gold that was boiling in the oil. A handful of hungry locals were in the queue ahead, but no one Bonnie knew. Still, they nodded and grunted their greetings in Bonnie's direction. That was a characteristic of this place that Bonnie sorely missed when he was up in the city. Nobody waved at you for the sake of waving. Some of the housemates made fun of him the first few weeks for throwing a friendly thumb towards confused drivers in passing cars. You'd be guaranteed a wave back once you broke off the main roads, but not a chance of it up above.

It wasn't even ten minutes by the time Bonnie was handed a warm brown paper bag over the silver countertop. Clued in enough to the goings-on of the place, Bonnie took a twenty out of his wallet instead of the card.

Hang onto the change sure. Bonnie pulled the bag from off the counter, waved his goodbye to Francis and slipped out the door. Darkness was falling in now causing the air to turn a hue of purple that confused the eyes. There was a bite of wind coming in but the bag of freshly fried food was warm against the thinness of Bonnie's torso. The walk home saw the darkness fully set in by the time Bonnie reached the farmhouse again. The dog barked a chorus of warnings before he picked up the familiar scent and bound toward Bonnie with a happy tail behind him.

The aul' fella was rubbing his hands in anticipation as Bonnie walked in the sliding door around the back.

Thanks be to Jaysus, Bon, I'm starved. The aul' man took the brown paper feast from Bonnie and started unpacking the food precariously onto plates that were waiting on the kitchen table. Been a fair minute since we've had Noreen's, lad. Your mudder says special occasions only now on account of my bloody cholesterol. In this hour of my life! He took a long chip into the gob and closed his eyes with the satisfaction of it. You'da sworn he'd not been fed in days. The mother bustled in from the darkness of the hallway.

Is he giving out again? You're a star, Bon, what do I owe ya? She was already sitting down to her share.

Don't worry about it, Ma, you've got it often enough. Bonnie slinked into the chair opposite the pair of them. The dull light of the kitchen lit them in a sombre glow, and Bonnie found himself wondering how many more years the pair of them had. They were old enough when they had him, much older than the parents of his friends. 'A surprise' was the nice way Mam put it to imply Bonnie was an unplanned error of a drunken stupor. Weren't we all mistakes to some degree anyway?

The thought caused an unchecked jolt of anxiety to moisten the palms of the farmer's son. He thought of the cold day that neither of his parents would exist anymore. Bonnie wondered if he'd have his own family by then and whether the pair before him would be grandparents before they took on. He wondered whether they'd be proud of him or ashamed on the final account. He knew they were traditional and conservative. He knew he himself was not, but that his difference had caused them to change in ways. Their minds had eased in their rigidity over the years at the challenge of their thoughtful son. It was hard to say by how much they had opened up, though.

The table was a quiet concentration as they gorged on the greasy wonder of the town's premier chipper. Saint threw his front paws up onto the table to investigate the possibility of some leftovers. A questioning groan indicated his disappointment, and he came away from the table to find the bowl containing his own, boring meal. The mudder cleared the table out of ingrained inclination, tidying up around the men of the house as the kettle boiled intrusively behind.

How are the women up above, so Bon? The aul' fella had a twinkle of mischief in his milky blue cornea. "There'd be all sorts roaming around that campus I reckon. He laughed at his own quip again, making eye contact with his son to ensure that the joke was indeed a funny one. Bonnie forced a make-shift chortle.

Martin Harrington, will you behave yourself! The mother gave her husband's shoulder a playful slap of the washcloth she was using to wipe down the table. Don't he have enough going on to be talking about that nonsense with you.

Wisht awhile so, Bon. We'll save that chat for the pub tomorrow evening. Be no jealous ears around then. He took a long glance at the mother for a reaction but none came. She knew well enough when to stop feeding the fire. Otherwise, he'd be at her all night. The tea was made and the chat revolved around the farm work or else they sat in familiar silence. Not long after ten, Bonnie said his good nights and went to his childhood bedroom to get some sleep. He'd try again tomorrow.

The fog rolled in off the river on business early on the Saturday morning at the bend of that black river. There'd be no heat in that sun above but it did its job to chase away the dense air by early afternoon. Bonnie wasn't seen in the gaf until about 12:45. The father slagged him as always on first sight.

Half the day is done and you only out of bed, hah? He allowed himself a good chuckle at himself again. Bonnie groaned good morning and flicked the kettle to boil. When he was away, he wanted to be home and when he was home he wanted to be away. The restlessness caused a palpable irritability that the aul' man was oblivious to. A deathly black coffee worked its way to perk Bonnie up. He spent the early afternoon sat at the kitchen table, trying to get his sociology essay half way started, but looking out the window of the back porch more than anything else to catch a glimpse of something more grounded.

At around the 4 o'clock mark, the dread of Saturday night pints with the father started seeping in. Sat in out of the way in the dingy back room of Bernie's wasn't exactly the night out Bonnie yearned for. Still, pints of stout out that end were as creamy as they come and it was the aul' fella's spot since time began the way he went on about it. It was a place for pensioner's and old lads with shaky hands and a distaste for harsh sunlight, mostly. You'd only get a woman in there during 12 pubs or the very odd depressing Hen-do on a pub crawl. The place had the demeanour of a forgotten living room inside a house that was barely lived in.

2 long-headed pints of an amber stout landed down on the table between them with a grunt of satisfaction from the aul' fella. The chair pushed back behind him ever so slightly to allow negotiation room for the gut. He still wore the work pants he'd on him all day. A move made out of laziness and to showcase a hard day's graft in equal parts. He'd a drinker's redness in the cheek and a bogman's round nose. There was always an air of mischief to his eyes though, and if you saw him coming toward you, you'd say he looked like a nice man.

There was welcoming chit-chat from the usuals as the aul' fella sat down. How's the wife, how's the crop; that sort of lark. Bonnie sat there in idle indifference. He'd given up on pretending he was the willing heir of the

Harrington farm a good while back, which was cause for many a week of minimal contact from the father. Still, the aul' fella knew his only son wasn't built for farming, and he'd made some version of peace with that.

Once Martin had finished his hellos and what have yous, he turned back and gazed at the now settled pints before him.

Chrisht, can you bate it, Bon? Look at those for me. He took up one of the drinks with the left paw and took a third of it in the one slug. Oh, yes, that's earned so it is.

It's not the same up in Cork, Da, I'll give you that. Bonnie's first sip was more polished, and he wiped the cream away from his lip habitually.

Tell me so, Bon, story with the women above? The question had burned a hole in Martin since the night before.

Ah, will you stop. I'm too busy, like. I, eh, I haven't the time on me to be chasing girls, Dad. Bonnie averted his glance and took in more stout. The heart was beating wildly under his shirt. Bonnie wondered if the aul' fella could see the fabric move in tune with his life rhythm.

Get out of that, boy. A fine-looking young fella like you. There'd be a line of them onto you, there always was when you were a young fella. I can respect a gent though, fair play. The aul' man tipped his pint to Bonnie and turned on his stool to take an eye to the rest of the bar. You could hardly say it was busy. Bonnie was relieved that the interrogation was short-lived and relaxed into himself. He was glad of the dimmed lights as he waited for his high cheeks to stop burning. The fire was lit over in the corner and there was some trad duo setting up on the far side of the bar. There'd be worse evening had in fairness.

By the time the father and son left Bernie's Pub, Bonnie had 6 pints in him and Martin had 9. The old farmer was a bit of a wobble on the gargle so Bonnie casually shouldered him to a taxi out on the curb. It was a walk they'd have managed if they'd called it at three pints but that was rarely the case. Martin lambasted the county council for the lack of road maintenance around the place and the driver nodded along politely, happy enough with the short fare. Bonnie sorted the cab fare as the aul' fella was already out the door and on the way to bed. He'd a tendency to be single-minded when the drink took effect. Bonnie went in, filled the dog's water bowl, and promptly passed out in his own room.

There'd been worse hangovers had. Bonnie rustled awake in a drunk fatigue just after 11. The aul' man was already up and into the work since 9. There'd be no days off had on the Harrington farm, hangover or not. Bonnie spotted him from the kitchen crossing the yard with a Pitbull's neck on him and a face fixed in response to a sun that wasn't there. Bonnie caught him by the fence into the cow's field and handed him a mug of coffee.

How's the head, Da? I've been better.

Ah tis fine, boy. Nothing I'm not used to at this hour of me life. He took a grateful slug of the coffee. Are you off, are you?

I am, yeah. Bus is leaving there at one, I'll be heading up along shortly. Was good to get back for a bit all the same.

Ah, you know you're welcome whenever you want. You might bring a young wan home to us, yet. Yer mudder be chuffed. Bonnie gave an apologetic smile to this father as a wave of guilt rose in him.

Well, I'll say goodbye to Mam and I'll be off. I'll buzz you during the week to see how ye're getting on. He lent in to give him aul' man a hug, which was a crooked and awkward affair. The guilt inside him broke and gave way to a shameful anger that he couldn't be honest with his father of all people.

He was on the bus and away by one. He'd reach the house down by the Maradyke and all by half three. The bus was up beyond Ballyvorney and all before Bonnie took a look at his phone. He'd been looking out the window in a thoughtless distance, not even seeing the passing countryside. Two texts in from Peter.

Well?

How'd it go? X

Bonnie stared at the screen. The line blinked back at him, waiting for a command, waiting for an answer. Both the line and Peter could wait. He threw the phone down beside him and began to star out the window once more.

About the Author

If you enjoyed this book, please consider leaving an online review. The author would appreciate reading your thoughts.

Visit the website at +

Subscribe to the newsletter at
+

You can also follow the author on social media
Instagram:
Twitter:
FaceBook:

About the Publisher

Sulis International Press publishes select fiction and nonfiction in a variety of genres under four imprints: Riversong Books, Sulis Academic Press, Sulis Press, and Keledei Publications.

For more, visit the website at
https://sulisinternational.com

Subscribe to the newsletter at
https://sulisinternational.com/subscribe/

Follow on social media
https://www.facebook.com/SulisInternational
https://twitter.com/Sulis_Intl
https://www.pinterest.com/Sulis_Intl/
https://www.instagram.com/sulis_international/

Printed in Great Britain
by Amazon